YORK NOTES

General Editors: Professor A.N. Jeffares (*University of Stirling*) & Professor Suheil Bushrui (*American University of Beirut*)

George Orwell

ANIMAL FARM

Notes by Robert Welch

MA (NUI) PH D (LEEDS)
Professor of English and Head of Department, Department of English, Media and Theatre Studies, University of Ulster at Coleraine

**LONGMAN
YORK PRESS**

YORK PRESS
Immeuble Esseily, Place Riad Solh, Beirut.

LONGMAN GROUP UK LIMITED
Longman House, Burnt Mill, Harlow,
Essex CM20 2JE, England
and Associated Companies throughout the World.

First published 1980
Sixth impression 1987

ISBN 0-582-78097-7

Produced by Longman Group (FE) Ltd
Printed in Hong Kong

Contents

Part 1

Introduction

ERIC ARTHUR BLAIR was born in 1903 in Motihari, in India. At the time India was part of the British Empire, and Blair's father held a post as agent in the Opium Department of the Indian Civil Service. Blair's paternal grandfather too had been part of the British Raj, and had served in the Indian Army. In 1907 the family returned to England and lived at Henley, though the father continued to work in India until he retired in 1912. His family's background in the British administration in India helps us to understand Blair's attitudes to the society into which he was born. In changing his name from Eric Blair to George Orwell later on in life, he was moving away quite deliberately from the relatively privileged and fairly pleasant existence the Blairs had enjoyed in helping to administer the Empire. Not that the Blair family were very wealthy – Orwell later described them ironically as 'lower-upper-middle-class'. They owned no property, had no extensive investments: they were like many middle-class families of the time, dependent on the Empire for their livelihood and prospects. Among the members of this class there was a continual attempt to better oneself, to move up the fairly rigid class system, and one way of helping one's children up the social ladder was to send them to good, expensive schools, traditionally associated with the upper class. Blair's parents sent the young Eric first to a private preparatory school in Sussex at the age of eight, and then, at the age of thirteen, he won a scholarship to Wellington, and soon after another scholarship to Eton, the famous public school.

On leaving Eton, Eric Blair joined the Indian Imperial Police. In doing so he was already breaking away from the path many of his school-fellows would take, where Eton led to either Oxford or Cambridge. Instead he was drawn to a life of travel and action. He trained in Burma, and served there for five years. In 1927, while home on leave, he resigned. There were two reasons (at least) for this: firstly, his life as a policeman in Burma was a distraction from the life he really wanted, which was to be a writer, and secondly, he had come to feel that as a policeman in Burma he was supporting a political system in which he could no longer believe. Even as early as this his ideas about writing and his political ideas were closely linked. But it wasn't simply that he wished to break away from his part in British imperialism in India; he wished 'to escape from . . . every form of man's dominion over man', as he said in *The Road to Wigan Pier* (p.130), and the social structure out of which he came depended, as he saw it, on just that 'dominion', not just over the Burmese, but over the English working class. Success in life, in the terms in which his family would understand success, seemed necessarily exploitation of the weak, both at home and abroad. So, failure, deliberate failure, turning one's back on one's family and one's inherited ideas and prejudices, seemed the only course open to a serious-minded man. In effect it meant that one would somehow have to take on a new identity and shed the old. This is exactly what Blair tried to do: he tried to change himself from Eric Blair, old Etonian and English colonial policeman, into George Orwell, classless anti-authoritarian. It will be clear, then, that Orwell's reasons for taking the name Orwell are much more complicated than those which writers usually have in mind when taking a pen name.

He turned his back on English imperialism and on his own inherited values by taking a drastic step. For the six months after his return from Burma he went to live among the poor in the East End of London. For him the English poor were the victims of injustice, playing the same part in England as the Burmese played in Burma. From being a servant of the British Empire he became a discoverer of his own country, and particularly of its working classes. The life he encountered in the East End was entirely outside his experience: the schools he had been to were all boarding schools, so he had been at home only in the holidays, and there he was protected from thinking about the less privileged by being brought up to believe that the working classes were somehow less than human, and, indeed, that they smelt. 'The lower classes smell', he tells us in *The Road to Wigan Pier* (p.112), was a phrase he used to hear quite often in his childhood. So in going to the East End of London he was overcoming a physical disgust against working people which he saw as typical of his class, but he was also trying to get rid of his own guilt for feeling in that way about other human beings. Did the English middle classes of the earlier part of this century believe that the working classes smelt like animals? It is doubtful if many of them did, but certainly Orwell was brought up to think so.

Having lived in the East End he then went to Paris, where he lived and worked in a working-class quarter of the city. At the time, he tells us, Paris was full of artists and would-be artists. It was 1928, and the franc was in a bad way, so that well-off foreigners could have a bohemian and artistic life fairly cheaply. But the life that Orwell led was far from bohemian; he worked (when he eventually found work) as a dishwasher in a Paris hotel. Once again his journey was downward into the life to which he felt he should expose himself, the life of the poverty-stricken, or of those who barely made a living.

In 1929 he returned to England, where he lived for a time as a tramp. He described his experiences in Paris and London in his first book, *Down and Out in Paris and London*, published in 1933. In the meantime he had taught, worked in a bookshop, and had done some journalism. *Down and Out in Paris and London* was not a novel; it was a documentary account of a life which not many contemporary middle-class readers would have sympathised with, in the way that Orwell did. And this was the point of it: he wished to bring the English middle classes, of which he was a member, to an understanding of what the life they led and enjoyed was founded upon, the life under their very noses. Here we see two of the most important aspects of Orwell as a writer: his idea of himself as the exposer of painful truths, at which people, for various reasons, do not wish to look; and his idea of himself as a representative of the English moral conscience. His idea of the writer as exposer of unpleasant truths, and as the moral conscience of the society in which he lives, is an old one, especially in English prose writing; it is the idea of John Bunyan, of Daniel Defoe, of Jonathan Swift, of George Crabbe and Thomas Carlyle. It is possible to see these two aspects of Orwell's writing combined in the intention that lies behind *Animal Farm*. How would you go about describing these two aspects at work there?

His next book was a novel, *Burmese Days*, published in 1934, and based on his experiences in the colonial service. This was followed by two more novels, *A Clergyman's Daughter*, published in 1935, and *Keep the Aspidistra Flying*, published in 1936. In 1936 he opened a village shop in Wallington, Hertfordshire, where he did business in the mornings, and wrote in the afternoons. In 1936 also, he married Eileen O'Shaughnessy. In that year he received a commission from the Left Book Club to do an examination into the condition of the poor and unemployed. This resulted in *The Road to Wigan Pier*, published in 1937. This inquiry was not a theoretical or philosophical one, which explained the condition of the working class in England by means of economic theories: it was an inquiry conducted along the same lines as Orwell's earlier journeys among the poor. He went to live among the people about whom he was going to write his book. Once again it is a journey away from the comparative comfort of middle-class life, made in order to find the truth of the situations he was to write about. He was an observer, keeping as fair-minded as possible about what he saw, remaining responsible to objective truth. His account of mining communities in the north of England in this book is full of detail, and conveys to the reader what it is actually like to go down a mine.

As a writer Orwell always had an immense respect for fact, for objective truth. When he saw this being threatened, for one reason or another, it disturbed him deeply. For Orwell one of the functions of a prose writer was to present facts as clearly as possible. 'Good prose is like a window-pane', he said in his essay 'Why I Write'. In other words writing should allow people to see clearly for themselves; it should never muddle or confuse. A writer should put down what he actually sees, not what he has been trained to see, or what a particular political line of thought might wish him to see. And, says Orwell, if a writer fails to do this, and lies about what he sees, his ability to write will dry up. He will become a tired hack if he allows someone else to dictate how the facts are to be seen. So, the freedom to see and think clearly is seen as absolutely fundamental to the writer, a freedom which political ideas of a too rigorous kind would try to hamper. The writer who holds on to this freedom to see things as they are, will, Orwell says, almost inevitably come into conflict with extreme political systems. The reader will see for himself this concern of Orwell's, that facts be truthfully and objectively reported, at work in *Animal Farm* on a number of occasions. He will see that in this book of Orwell's it is frequently convenient for those who have taken power, to distort the truth of what has happened, even to revise the past. It might be useful to make a list of occasions in the story when facts are adjusted to new sets of circumstances.

It was the writer's duty, then, as Orwell saw it, to keep his eyes open, to keep his prose simple and direct, and to try and free himself from prejudice, inherited or political. When the Left Book Club read what he had written about the English class system and English socialism* in *The Road to Wigan Pier*, they were not pleased, and when the book was published it contained a preface by Victor Gollancz taking issue with most of Orwell's important points.

The first half of the book vividly describes the conditions of working-class life in the town of Wigan, and this vividness comes from the sense we have of Orwell as a trustworthy guide. This trust is carried over to the second half of the book which is, in fact, an attack on English socialism of his own time. Basing his argument on personal experience, commonsense, but mostly on observed fact, Orwell comes to the conclusion that the socialism of his time was mostly unrealistic and irrelevant. Socialism tended to be middle-class and had very little idea of how the workers lived or how they thought, because the class barriers cannot be so easily wiped out. The kind of socialist Orwell makes fun of is the sort who spouts phrases like 'proletarian solidarity', wears sandals, and burbles about 'dialectical materialism', and in so doing has the effect of putting ordinary decent people off, the people for whom Orwell wishes to speak, the people whom, as the book itself shows, he has taken considerable trouble to get to know. Before

*Socialism: the political and economic theory that the wealth of a people should belong to the people, that everyone should be equal, and that there should be security for all.

socialism can become a real possibility, and not just a theoretical amusement for cranks, the class divisions in English society will have to go, but they will have to go slowly, they are so deeply ingrained. There is, though, a strong sense in the book, that the class differences may not go at all, or may just simply reappear as another form of oppression, a sense that there may be something in human nature which divides society into ruler and ruled. The differences between ruler and ruled are so great as to suggest that they belong to a different species, or as if the rulers were humans, the workers animals (to employ the imagery of *Animal Farm*). It may sometimes happen that the ruled will topple the oppressors, but very soon new tyrants will rise to replace the old. Throughout Orwell's writing there is the sense that there is something vitally wrong with human nature, despite the dreams men have of ideal societies, or Utopias. You could comment on this with regard to *Animal Farm*.

Orwell was asked by the Left Book Club to do *The Road to Wigan Pier* because he was a socialist, but as will be clear his socialism was of a very personal, individual kind. In a way his socialism was a continuation into the twentieth century of the Protestant English moral tradition.

Having completed *The Road to Wigan Pier* he went to Spain at the end of 1936, with the idea of writing newspaper articles on the Civil War which had broken out there. The conflict in Spain was between the Communist, Socialist Republic, and General Franco's Fascist military Rebellion. (See definitions at end of section.) When he arrived in Barcelona he was astonished at the atmosphere he found there: what had seemed impossible in England seemed a fact of daily life in Spain. Class distinction seemed to have vanished. There was a shortage of everything, but there was equality. Orwell joined in the struggle, by enlisting in the militia of the POUM (Partido Obrero de Unification Marxista), with which the British Independent Labour Party had an association. For the first time in his life socialism seemed a reality, something worth fighting for. And fight he did. By January 1937 he was in action on the Aragon front. He was wounded in the throat. Three and a half months later, when he returned to Barcelona, he found it a changed city. No longer a place where the socialist word 'comrade' was really felt to mean something, it was a 'city returning to normal', with the workers no longer 'in the saddle'. Worse, he was to find that the group he was with, the POUM, was now accused of being a Fascist militia, secretly helping Franco. Orwell had to sleep in the open for fear of showing his papers, and eventually managed to escape into France with his wife. His account of his days in Spain was published in *Homage to Catalonia* in 1938.

His experiences in Spain left two impressions on Orwell's mind: firstly, they showed him that socialism in action was a human possibility, if only a temporary one. He never forgot the exhilaration of those first days in Barcelona, where a new society seemed possible, where the word 'comradeship', instead of being a political term, became a reality for him. But secondly, the experience of the city returning to normal he saw as a gloomy confirmation of the idea we have met before, that there is something in human nature that seeks violence, conflict, power over others. It will be clear that these two impressions, of hope on the one hand, and of despair on the other, are entirely contradictory. Nevertheless, despite the despair and confusion of his return to Barcelona (there were street fights between different groups of socialists), the overall impression his time in Spain left him with was a hopeful one. At the end, while preparing to leave Spain, he was able to say 'I have seen wonderful things, and at last really believe in socialism'. The ordinary decent people of Spain were capable of uniting to oppose the power that would try to oppress them. But as time went on Orwell's view of things was to darken, and he developed an overwhelming sense of the futility of man's efforts to improve his lot. Can the reader see evidence of this increasing despair in *Animal Farm*? Is the whole book just one long moan of hopelessness? Clearly it is not. Why not?

When looking at the puzzling question of Orwell's differing attitudes to socialism, it is well to remember that the period in which he was learning his craft as a writer, the 1930s, was the decade when Hitler and Mussolini came to power, the decade of Fascism*. Hitler called the Nazi party a Nationalist Socialist party, an example of the abuse and distortion of language for political ends that disgusted Orwell so much. And yet, it seemed to Orwell and to many writers of the time, among them W.H. Auden, Stephen Spender, Louis MacNeice and Christopher Isherwood, that some form of socialism, which would protect the individual, and his freedom to see things for himself, was the only defence against the advancing Fascist armies. The only trouble was, as Orwell pointed out in *The Road to Wigan Pier*, that socialism itself was inclined to insist on its own way of seeing things, and to insist that the writer should suppress his own view of things when they were in conflict with what the party thought. This for Orwell was the end of a writer as a creative artist, because creativity was first and foremost for Orwell a matter of being able to see things for oneself. Because socialism often considered that a possible danger to the movement, Orwell came to feel that socialism could easily have a kind of Fascism inside it, waiting to spring on the party member who dared to be different. To Orwell the freedom to be different within

---

*Fascism: in some ways the opposite ideology to socialism. It is authoritarian, strongly nationalist and believes in force as a means of getting its way. Founded by Benito Mussolini in Italy in 1919.

one's society was all important. This feature of socialism, of having an inbuilt Fascism inside it, can be seen in *Animal Farm*, in the way the Socialist Revolution against the humans gives way to a Fascist dictatorship under the pigs.

In 1938 Orwell became ill with tuberculosis, and spent the winter in Morocco. While there he wrote his next book, a novel entitled *Coming Up for Air*, published in 1939, the year the long-threatened war between England and Germany broke out. Here the enemy was very clearly a Fascist one and Orwell wanted to fight, as he had done in Spain, but was declared unfit. In 1941 he joined the BBC as talks producer in the Indian section of the Eastern Service. He served in the Home Guard, a wartime civilian body for local defence. In 1943 he left the BBC to become literary editor of *Tribune*, and began writing *Animal Farm*. The difficulties of living during wartime, with its shortage of food and other essentials, undoubtedly influenced the story's atmosphere of gloom. In 1944 the Orwells adopted a son, but in 1945 his wife died during an operation. Towards the end of the war Orwell went to Europe as a reporter.

Late in 1945 he went to the island of Jura off the Scottish coast, and settled there in 1946. It was an unsuitable place for someone suffering from TB to live. At Jura he wrote *Nineteen Eighty-Four* (1949). In that year he married Sonia Brownell. He died in January 1950.

Summary

These points should be borne in mind when studying *Animal Farm*:

(1) Orwell left his own background to discover the England he did not know, working-class England.
(2) As a writer he regarded himself as the exposer of unpleasant truths about society, and as the voice of the English moral conscience. These two aspects were tied in with his brand of socialism.
(3) Good writers should see the facts as they are, not as someone else might like them to be. For this reason writing involved politics for Orwell.
(4) Orwell thought there was something fundamentally wrong with human nature, something idealistic political systems tended to overlook.
(5) Orwell felt that socialism could have a kind of Fascism inside it.

A note on the text

Animal Farm was first published by Secker and Warburg Limited of London in 1945. It was published by Penguin Books Limited, Harmondsworth, in 1951, and has been reprinted many times since.

Part 2

Summaries
of ANIMAL FARM

A general summary

There is a rebellion on Manor Farm, and the animals seize power from Mr Jones, the lazy owner. All animals are to be equal, and human ways are banned. The pigs, being the most intelligent of the animals, take control of the organisation of the farm. At their head are Napoleon and Snowball. The pigs, however, treat themselves much better than they do the other animals; the other animals are told that this is necessary, seeing that pigs do all the brainwork.

Other animals on neighbouring farms hear of the rebellion on Animal Farm, and this begins to worry the nearby farmers. Led by Jones, a group of them attempt to take the farm back, but they are defeated in the Battle of the Cowshed, led by Snowball. After this Snowball plans to build a windmill to supply electricity but is opposed by Napoleon. At one of the Sunday meetings held to celebrate the rebellion, Snowball, having persuaded the animals of the value of the windmill, is put to flight by nine dogs which Napoleon has secretly reared. When Snowball is gone the windmill is said to have been Napoleon's idea all the time, and it is to be built.

Napoleon begins to trade with the village, and the pigs move into the farmhouse, contrary to the first principles of the Revolution. A storm comes and blows the partly-built windmill down, but Snowball is blamed for this. The second winter comes in and food supplies run short, but Napoleon makes the outside world believe that there is plenty on Animal Farm. Napoleon decides that Snowball had been Jones's secret agent all the time, and Squealer, Napoleon's information officer, puts it about that it was Napoleon who led the animals to victory in the Battle of the Cowshed. Boxer, the faithful work-horse, queries this, but is silenced by Squealer's firmness. Snowball is supposed to be getting into the farm at night-time and spreading treachery. One day pigs, hens, a goose and some others come forward and 'confess' to having committed crimes against the farm, urged on by Snowball. They are all slaughtered in public.

One by one the original Commandments of Animalism are altered to fit in with what Napoleon wishes to do. Eventually the windmill is finished and timber is sold to Frederick, one of the neighbouring farmers, to buy machinery. Frederick pays in forged money, then

attacks the farm and blows up the windmill. The animals manage to
defeat Frederick and his men, but a number of them are killed. This is
called the Battle of the Windmill. The pigs grow more and more
corrupt, and take to drink. Napoleon becomes an increasingly
merciless dictator. Boxer's great energy at last gives out, but after
years of tireless work, instead of being retired on a 'pension' he is sent
to the knacker's yard.

Years pass. The pigs end up looking just like the human beings they
once replaced. They walk on their hind legs, carry whips, and invite
the neighbours round for dinner. At last the name of Animal Farm is
changed back to Manor Farm.

Detailed summaries

Chapter 1

When the book opens it is night-time on Manor Farm. Mr Jones, the
owner, is drunk as usual. When the lights in the house go out all the
animals gather in the big barn, where old Major, the prize Middle
White boar, is to address them. We are introduced to the animals on
the farm as they come in: the dogs; the two carthorses, Boxer and
Clover; Muriel the goat; Benjamin the donkey; the hens and ducklings,
and Mollie, the pretty but foolish white mare. Major has gathered
them together to pass on the wisdom he has learnt in a long life. This
wisdom is that:

(1) Man is the only enemy the animals have. He 'consumes without
    producing', he uses the animals to maintain his high standard of
    living, and yet gives them practically nothing in return.
(2) All animals are killed in the end. The young porkers will scream
    their lives out on the block within the year, Boxer will, in the end,
    be brought to the knacker's. The dogs will be drowned.
(3) The only solution lies in rebellion against Man. Major is not sure
    when it will come, but come it surely must.
(4) 'All men are enemies. All animals are comrades', Major says. They
    must never come to resemble Man. They must never adopt any of
    his corrupt habits, such as sleeping in a bed, wearing clothes, or
    drinking alcohol.
(5) Not only are all animals comrades, but all animals are equal. No
    animal must ever kill any other animal.
(6) Finally Major sings them a song that had come back to him in a
    dream the previous night: it is called 'Beasts of England', and
    looks forward to the day when Man and his ways will be gone
    forever, when the 'golden future time' will have arrived.

All the animals sing the song and the din awakens Jones, who thinks there must be a fox in the yard. He shoots his shotgun into the darkness, the animals disperse quickly and quietly settle down.

COMMENTARY: The first paragraph of the story sets the atmosphere of Manor Farm very effectively. Jones is drunk, and forgets to shut the pop-holes of the hen-houses for the night, thus leaving the hens at the mercy of foxes, or indeed rats. He is a careless farmer, and does not take his duties seriously. In Orwell's story he stands for the lazy, privileged upper classes, those who control wealth and exploit others. The animals stand for those who are exploited. They are the working classes in general, *and* they are the Russian peasants before the Revolution, just as Jones is the ruling class in general *and* the Russian Czar as well. Orwell is simplifying the issues, of course, but is doing so in order to gain clarity and intensity. Old Major could be said to stand for a combination of Karl Marx, Friedrich Engels (the two great nineteenth-century theorists of socialism) and Vladimir Ilich Lenin, leader of the Bolshevik Revolution of 1917. His speech is a wonderfully concise account of Marxist socialist theory. The idealistic nature of this theory is cleverly pointed to in the tiny episode of the rats. While Major is speaking four rats appear from their holes and the dogs rush at them. Major says that it should be put to the vote whether the rats be considered comrades or not. The vote is that the rats are comrades, even though throughout the tale they give trouble. Here, Orwell, at the very beginning of the story, would seem to be implying that certain creatures have certain natures, and that despite votes and idealistic resolutions, very little can be done about it.

NOTES AND GLOSSARY:
tushes: long pointed teeth

Chapter 2

Early in March old Major dies, and after his death the pigs teach and organise Rebellion. Chief among the pigs are two boars, Snowball and Napoleon. Snowball is more alert and lively than Napoleon, but the latter has a reputation for getting his own way. The rest of the male pigs are porkers (castrated pigs) and the best known among them is Squealer, a brilliant talker and persuader. These three develop Major's ideas into a complete system of thought and they call this 'Animalism'. They explain the principles of this system to the animals, but some of them have difficulty grasping it. Mollie, for example, asks if she will be allowed to wear ribbons after the Rebellion, but it is explained to her that ribbons are a sign of her slavery. The pigs also have difficulty dealing with Moses the raven, who tells the animals stories about

Sugarcandy Mountain, a place beyond the clouds where all animals go after they die. There, according to Moses, it is Sunday all the week and sugar and linseed cake grow on the hedges. The pigs work hard at convincing the animals that Moses is telling lies. Boxer and Clover faithfully accept what the pigs tell them and pass it on to the others.

Quite suddenly one day the Rebellion comes. Jones goes into the village, Willingdon, on a Saturday, and then falls asleep, forgetting to feed the animals. By evening the animals are starving and at last a cow breaks down the door of the store shed with her horns. The animals then begin to feed themselves. Jones wakes up and he and his men (who have been rabbiting) try to control the animals. They fight back, and rout Jones and his men. Mrs Jones slips out by a back way. The farm now belongs to the animals.

Firstly, they burn the signs of their slavery, the nose-rings, dog-chains, knives, reins, halters and so on. In celebration Napoleon serves out a double ration of corn to each one. Next morning they look over the farm and can hardly believe that it now belongs to them. They inspect the farmhouse and are amazed at its luxury. They decide that it is to be a museum and that no animal must ever live there. The pigs (who have been teaching themselves how to read and write) change the name of the farm on the gate from Manor Farm to Animal Farm. They then go back to the big barn and on its side the pigs paint the Seven Commandments of Animalism. These Seven Commandments are to be an 'unalterable law':

(1) Whatever goes upon two legs is an enemy.
(2) Whatever goes upon four legs, or has wings, is a friend.
(3) No animal shall wear clothes.
(4) No animal shall sleep in a bed.
(5) No animal shall drink alcohol.
(6) No animal shall kill any other animal.
(7) All animals are equal.

The cows have not been milked as yet, so the pigs manage to do it with their trotters. Someone asks what is to happen to the milk and Napoleon tells them not to mind about it. They go off to get the harvest in and when they return they notice that the milk has gone.

COMMENTARY: Here three main things happen: firstly the organisation of old Major's ideas into a system by the boars Napoleon and Snowball, and the porker Squealer; secondly the expounding of that system by the pigs and the reactions to it of the different animals; thirdly, the Rebellion itself, and the events following it.

We also notice here how Orwell gives his 'fairy story' a sense of being rooted in real things. He is concerned that his fable should not become too theoretical, so preoccupied with politics as to lose the reader's interest. One of the means he uses to keep the reader's interest is emphasising details that are not entirely necessary to his meaning.

The student might well go through this chapter carefully, noting those details which are used to bring the story to life, and to give this basically incredible tale reality. Examples might be Squealer's 'twinkling eyes'; Jones's habit of feeding the raven with bits of bread dipped in beer; the detail about Jones falling asleep with *The News of the World* over his face. Orwell uses such non-essential details throughout. The reader should be on the look-out for them.

A curious thing in this chapter is the episode dealing with Moses the raven, who is Jones's pet, and who tells the animals about Sugarcandy Mountain, and in so doing distracts the animals from the purity of Animalism. Clearly Moses is intended to be a satire on religion and the clergy, the raven's black coat being appropriate for this. Also, like his biblical namesake, he speaks of the promised land. He changes sides when the Rebellion comes, then disappears for most of the book.

The Rebellion stands for the Bolshevik Revolution of November 1917 in Russia, led by Lenin. 'Animalism' is Orwell's translation into animal terms of Communist Socialism, based on the *Communist Manifesto* of 1848, written by Marx and Engels. The *Manifesto* was an inspiration for socialist thought throughout the latter part of the nineteenth century, and was a driving force behind the Bolshevik Revolution of 1917. The *Manifesto* was also the inspiration for Orwell's 'Seven Commandments'.

By the end of the chapter we are aware that Napoleon is looking after himself, that power has begun to corrupt.

NOTES AND GLOSSARY:
knoll: a small hill
spinney: a small wood
lithograph: a print made with an etched stone

Chapter 3

The harvest is a great success, despite difficulties in handling the tools designed for humans. All the animals work with a will; the pigs, of course, supervise. Boxer, the workhorse, is devoted to the Rebellion; his motto is, 'I will work harder'. Mollie, the mare, is inclined to shirk, and Benjamin, the donkey, remains unchanged. Each Sunday morning the flag of the future Republic of the Animals is raised and 'Beasts of England' is sung. Snowball is very concerned about education and sets up various committees. He tries to teach the animals to write and has some success but ability varies so much that he eventually reduces the Seven Commandments to one, which everyone can easily remember, even the sheep; 'Four legs good, two legs bad'. This, Snowball says, contains the essence of Animalism.

Napoleon takes little interest in Snowball's re-education plans; to his mind it is much more important to educate the young. So, when the dogs Jessie and Bluebell produce a large litter of nine puppies he takes them away to a loft and says he will be responsible for their education. Everyone else forgets about the puppies, but later on they are to play a significant part in Napoleon's dictatorship.

It is autumn and the apples begin to fall in the orchard. The animals think that they are to be shared out equally among them but they, like the milk, are to be set aside for the use of the pigs only. Squealer, who is Napoleon's information officer, explains that pigs need apples and milk because they are brain-workers. It is for the sake of the other animals that they eat them, not because they enjoy them. If the pigs failed in their duty then Jones would come back.

COMMENTARY: At first all goes well with the Rebellion. Everything runs fairly smoothly in this chapter, although Orwell's irony is apparent throughout. If Orwell has a spokesman in this book it is Benjamin the donkey, who remains unimpressed by the Rebellion. Boxer's simple devotion, however, to its ideals, is touching.

Orwell also has fun with Snowball's re-education plans, and with the obviously silly names of the committees he sets up, the 'Clean Tails League' for the cows, for example. Also, Snowball's reduction of the Commandments of Animalism for the benefit of the stupider animals, and the way the sheep mindlessly take it up, parodies the way socialist ideology reduces itself to simple formulas that everyone can understand but which stop any kind of thought. In the *Communist Manifesto*, for example, there is the following sentence: 'The theory of the Communists may be summed up in the single sentence: Abolition of private property'. Set this beside the basic principle of Animalism: 'Four legs good, two legs bad', and Orwell's feelings about the dangers of oversimplification are clear. Orwell regards any kind of slogan as intellectually damaging, and is criticising socialism for what he sees as its tendency in this direction.

The pigs are seen to be more and more greedy as the tale goes on.

NOTES AND GLOSSARY:
windfalls: apples blown down by the autumn winds

Chapter 4

There are two farms adjoining Animal Farm, Foxwood, owned by Pilkington, and Pinchfield, owned by Frederick. They are nearly always on bad terms with each other, but are both frightened by the Rebellion. Their animals come to hear of it, and in fact throughout the countryside the song of Rebellion, 'Beasts of England', can be heard everywhere. Frederick and Pilkington put out false rumours about Animal Farm, saying that it is a wicked and unnatural place.

Early in October, when the corn is cut and stacked, Jones, aided by men from Foxwood and Pinchfield, makes an attack on the farm. The animals, led by Snowball, defeat them, by means of a carefully worked out defence. Snowball (who is wounded by Jones's gun) and Boxer both fight very bravely. Napoleon is noticeable by his absence. A sheep is killed and she is given a solemn funeral; Snowball and Boxer are awarded a newly-created military decoration, 'Animal Hero, First Class'. The battle is to be remembered as the Battle of the Cowshed.

COMMENTARY: The main features of this chapter are the introduction of the two adjoining farms into the story, and the Battle of the Cowshed. In Orwell's fable Foxwood stands for Britain and Pinchfield for Germany. Pilkington is easy-going and careless, Frederick shrewd and hard-working. They disagree but join together to try to get Jones back his farm; they do this because what has happened on Animal Farm could also happen to them. What happened in Russia may also happen in the rest of Europe.

Chapter 5

Mollie the mare, having become more and more troublesome, eventually leaves Animal Farm: the work and the fact that there are no humans to make a fuss of her do not suit her. The pigeons tell the animals that they have seen her in Willingdon with a scarlet ribbon around her forelock. The winter comes round again, and, whereas last winter the time was spent on re-education committees and the like, this winter there is much conflict over policy. Snowball wants to industrialise the farm and to make it more efficient by means of field-drains and fertilisation methods. Napoleon disagrees with everything Snowball suggests, especially with what he has to say about a plan for a windmill.

Snowball maintains that a windmill would supply the farm with electricity, and that electricity would make the work of the farm much easier, giving the animals much more time for leisure. Napoleon says that food production is most important, and that if they waste time building a windmill they will starve to death. The animals divide into two groups, one backing Snowball, the other Napoleon. Eventually the matter is to be decided by vote at one of the Sunday meetings. Snowball stands up and makes a speech describing the benefits of the windmill; Napoleon gets up and says very quietly that the whole idea is nonsense. Snowball again gets up in passionate defence of his idea, and it is quite clear that if it goes to a vote Snowball will win. At this point Napoleon makes a strange highpitched whimper, and the nine puppies he has educated bound in and attack Snowball. He flees and just escapes with his life.

Napoleon now announces that the Sunday meetings will come to an end, that the pigs will decide all policy and communicate it to the animals, without discussion. Four young porkers squeal their disapproval, but at a growl from the dogs they shut up. Later on, when Squealer comes round to explain the expulsion of Snowball, someone remembers his bravery at the Battle of the Cowshed. Squealer replies that loyalty and obedience are much more important than bravery and that anyway time will show that his place in the Battle was much exaggerated. Discipline, he says, is what is needed. If they do not have that then Jones will come back. The animals again find this argument unanswerable.

Three weeks later it is announced that the windmill is to be built after all. Squealer is again sent round to explain the decision. It appears from what he says that the windmill was Napoleon's idea from the start, that he had seemed to oppose it in order to get rid of Snowball who was a bad influence. He calls this 'tactics'. The animals do not know what this word means, but Squealer whisks his tail so persuasively, and the dogs that now accompany him everywhere growl so fiercely, that they accept what he says.

COMMENTARY: The pig regime continues to tighten in this chapter. Napoleon is jealous of Snowball's popularity and his success as a speaker. In the fable Napoleon stands for Josef Stalin, and Snowball for Leon Trotsky. After Lenin died in 1924, Stalin was general secretary of the Communist Party in Russia, Trotsky was commissar for war. Between then and 1927, when Trotsky was sent into exile, he and Stalin disagreed violently over policy. Stalin wanted to concentrate on agriculture, where Trotsky wanted to industrialise (the debate over the windmill). The dogs stand for Stalin's dreaded secret police. With the dogs behind him Napoleon stops the Sunday morning debates; having got rid of Snowball he now begins to become a dictator. One of the things he does immediately is to attempt to gain control over what people think. Having believed all along that Napoleon did not approve of the windmill for what they thought were sincere reasons, they now have to accept the absurdity that he does. The dogs get them to accept this absurdity by growling. Fear, Orwell would appear to think, can make people accept as consistent what they know to be inconsistent. This is a major theme of his last book, *Nineteen Eighty-Four*, the book he wrote after *Animal Farm*.

Again Orwell's irony is at work here: the dogs wag their tails to Napoleon in the same way as they used to wag them to Jones. Have things changed very much? This is one of the questions the book asks.

NOTES AND GLOSSARY:

incubator: a heated machine for hatching eggs artificially

Chapter 6

Throughout the spring and summer the animals work like slaves, consoled by the thought that they are working for themselves. Despite this it is obvious that the coming year is to be a hard one. They start work on the windmill, but it is a slow business, as they have to drag the stones up the slope of the quarry and then smash them to bits by dropping them over the edge. Boxer excels himself and puts all his energy into the task. They have no more food than they did in Jones's day, but it seems to them that they do not have less. One Sunday Napoleon announces that he now intends to engage in trade with the neighbouring farmers, not for profit but for materials necessary to the windmill. The animals are a bit uneasy about this: they seem to remember something in their original resolutions about not engaging in trade with humans. The four porkers who objected to Napoleon's abolition of the Sunday debate protest again but they are silenced by growls from the dogs. Napoleon reveals that a Mr Whymper will act as agent for the farm. Afterwards Squealer makes another of his tours to explain the latest policy, and says that they may have dreamed that there was a resolution about not engaging in trade with humans. It is imagination, he says, traceable to lies put about by Snowball.

The humans have, in fact, developed a kind of admiration for the efficiency of the farm. There are constant rumours that Napoleon is about to enter into an agreement with either Pilkington or Frederick, but never both at once. The pigs move into the house at this stage. Again Squealer convinces the animals that it is only right that the Leader (as Napoleon is now called) should live in a house. They also find out that the pigs sleep in the beds. This disturbs some of the animals. Clover gets Muriel the goat to read the Fourth Commandment, and this now reads 'No animal shall sleep in a bed *with sheets*'. She cannot remember anything about sheets in the original Commandment, but she supposes it must have been there.

By November the windmill is half-built, but one night a violent storm blows up and in the morning they find the windmill in pieces. Napoleon snuffles around and announces that it is Snowball who is responsible for the sabotage. He resolves that they shall start again, and show the traitor that they cannot be discouraged.

COMMENTARY: After the dogs frighten the four porkers who object to engaging in trade with humans into silence there is an awkward moment. The sheep cover this by bawling out the mindless slogan of Animalism, 'Four legs good, two legs bad'. They do this at difficult moments throughout the book, as if they sense the difficulty and then try to drown out any possibility of thought.

Also in this chapter, we see an example of how political power, as Orwell sees it, is prepared to alter the past in people's minds if the past prevents it from doing what it wishes to do. Here the Fourth Commandment is altered in order that the pigs can sleep comfortably in warm beds. A simple addition of two words to the original Commandment does it. When the storm blows down the half-built windmill Napoleon insists that it is Snowball who is at fault. If it were admitted that the storm blew the structure down, the animals might get to thinking that perhaps the walls were not thick enough in the first place. Napoleon is beginning to determine how the animals see things, is beginning to control the truth, and to manipulate it to his own benefit.

NOTES AND GLOSSARY:
ignominious: humiliated

Chapter 7

It is a bad winter. They start to rebuild the windmill but now the walls are three feet thick. In January food falls short, but the pigs pretend to the outside world that there is plenty on the farm. As time goes on, however, it becomes obvious that something will have to be done. One Sunday morning Squealer announces that the hens will have to produce four hundred eggs a week. They protest, and something like a Rebellion takes place. Led by three Black Minorca pullets they fly up to the rafters and drop their eggs to the floor. For five days they are starved of rations, at which point they give in. Nine hens die in the siege.

All this while there is no sign of Snowball. Sometimes he is rumoured to be staying at Foxwood, at other times to be at Pinchfield. It is announced that Snowball has been visiting the farm at night, spreading treason, and generally doing mischief. Anything that goes wrong is blamed on Snowball. The rats, who have been troublesome, are said to be in league with him. At last it is decided that Snowball has gone over to Frederick and that they are plotting to overthrow the farm. It is even revealed that he had been in league with Jones from the start, and that he attempted to have the animals defeated at the Battle of the Cowshed. At this, Boxer, who very rarely asks questions, is puzzled. Was Snowball not wounded? Had he not been decorated?

Squealer explains all this as part of the arrangement between Jones and Snowball. Napoleon is said to have saved the day by biting Jones's leg. He then clinches it by saying that comrade Napoleon says so. This satisfies Boxer.

Four days later all the animals are gathered together in the yard. At a signal from Napoleon the dogs bound forward and drag out the four porkers that have protested in the past. They then, to everybody's surprise attack Boxer, but he fights them off without difficulty. Napoleon orders him to let the dog he is holding under his hoof go. The four porkers then confess they have been in league with Snowball since he left. Their throats are torn out by the dogs after they have confessed. The three pullets who led the hen Rebellion are also killed after they too have confessed to being influenced by Snowball. Other animals confess, and are slaughtered.

After the scenes of blood the animals go to the knoll where the windmill is being rebuilt. They are sad, and Boxer resolves to work even harder. This, and 'Napoleon is always right', is his answer to every difficulty. Clover, however, thinks to herself that this is not what they got rid of Jones for. They sing 'Beasts of England' three times. Squealer then comes up to them and tells them that the song is abolished. It expressed longing for a better time, he explains, but now that better time has come. Instead they have a new song composed by Minimus, the pig poet.

COMMENTARY: In this chapter Napoleon's dictatorship shows its disregard for the facts and its merciless brutality. In the first place the animals have to accept, because Napoleon says so, that Snowball was a traitor on the day of the Battle of the Cowshed, despite the fact that they remember otherwise. Secondly they witness the forced confessions and the executions. Even Boxer is attacked. Why? When they go to the grassy knoll where the windmill is being built Clover thinks back on Major's speech before he died, and thinks how far they have gone from what he would have intended. The reader should also remind himself of old Major's speech in Chapter 1 and compare it with what has happened in this important chapter. In doing so he will be contrasting the ideals of Communist Socialism with how Orwell saw Stalinist Russia debasing those ideals.

NOTES AND GLOSSARY:

cannibalism: the practice of eating one's own kind
infanticide: the murder of an infant
coccidiosis: a contagious infection of birds and animals

Chapter 8

A few days after the executions some of the animals think they remember that one of the Commandments read 'No animal shall kill any other animal'. Once again Muriel reads the Commandments from the barn wall and finds that the Sixth now reads 'No animal shall kill any other animal, *without cause*'. They do not remember the last bit but all are agreed that there was good cause for killing the traitors. Napoleon now has a black cockerel who goes before him as a kind of trumpeter. The pigs invent rather grand titles for him, such as 'Father of All Animals', or 'Ducklings' Friend'. All good luck is now said to come from him.

Meanwhile, through Whymper, Napoleon is engaged in business negotiations with Frederick and Pilkington about the sale of a pile of timber left over from Jones's day. Snowball is still said to be on Frederick's farm, and there are rumours that Frederick wishes to destroy the windmill. Relations with Pilkington become almost friendly. Stories about Frederick's cruelty to animals go about and the animals boil with rage against him. One Sunday Napoleon announces that he had never thought of selling the pile of timber to Frederick.

By the autumn the windmill is finished and it is named Napoleon Mill. They need machinery, and then one day they are told that the timber has been sold to Frederick. They are amazed, but it is explained that all the time Napoleon, by pretending to be friendly towards Pilkington, had been misleading Frederick. By this trick he got Frederick to raise his offer by twelve pounds. Napoleon has insisted on cash. Three days later it turns out that the notes Frederick gave them are forgeries. The next morning Frederick attacks with fifteen men. The attackers cannot be stopped so easily this time. Frederick's men, in fact, blow up the newly-finished windmill. At this the animals attack and drive the men off, but there are heavy casualties. The Battle is to be called the Battle of the Windmill.

A few days later the pigs find a case of whisky in the cellar of the house, and they all get drunk. Napoleon is seen galloping round the yard with a bowler hat on his head. Next day it is put about that Comrade Napoleon is dying. As his last act upon earth Napoleon has decreed that drinking alcohol is to be punished by death. However, as the days wear on he recovers, and a week later, it becomes known that the paddock beyond the orchard, which was to be a grazing ground for retired animals, is to be ploughed up and planted with barley for brewing. One night there is a loud crash, and when the animals go out they find Squealer sprawling on the ground near where the Seven Commandments are written, a broken ladder beside him and a spilled pot of white paint. The animals, apart from Benjamin, do not understand what has happened. Next day they find that the Fifth Commandment is yet another Commandment which they seem to have remembered wrongly. It now reads 'No animal shall drink alcohol *to excess*'.

COMMENTARY: Much of what happens in this chapter cannot be understood if we do not remember that Foxwood stands for England and Pinchfield for Germany. The differing attitudes of Napoleon towards them stand for the differing attitudes of Stalin towards the French and English allies and the German Nazis. The rumours of Frederick's cruelty are the rumours of Hitler's cruelty to the Jews in the 1930s. And then, amazingly, despite these stories Napoleon trades with Frederick, just as Stalin's Communist Russia sided with Hitler to everyone's astonishment in 1939. Of course Animal Farm is deceived by Frederick (Hitler), and his attack on the farm stands for Hitler's invasion of the Soviet Union, his supposed ally, in 1941.

The pigs grow more and more corrupt, breaking yet another Commandment of the Rebellion, and then adjusting it as they have done before. The animals seem to grow more and more incapable of thinking for themselves. Even when they see Squealer lying on the ground with the tin of paint, they still fail to realise what is happening. The only one who actually understands what is going on is Benjamin, and he says nothing.

NOTES AND GLOSSARY:

Crown Derby: expensive chinaware made at Derby in England, often marked with a crown surmounting a D

Chapter 9

The day after the Battle of the Windmill the animals start rebuilding it again. Boxer has only one ambition, to see the windmill well under way again by the time he retires. Seeing that the paddock beyond the orchard (which was to be set aside for retired animals) is to be used for barley, there is a rumour that a corner of the large pasture is to be used instead. Boxer's twelfth birthday, the agreed retiring age for horses, is due next summer.

Life is hard. This winter is as cold as the last one, rations are even shorter, and are reduced again for everyone save the pigs and dogs. But the animals are free, as Squealer does not fail to point out, and they are much better off than they ever were in the time of Jones. There are many more to feed now as well, as all four sows have littered, producing thirty-one pigs. Napoleon is the father of all of them. These piglets are discouraged from playing with the other animals.

The pigs start brewing their own beer. They hold Spontaneous Demonstrations every week, the purpose of which is to remind the animals how lucky they are to be on Animal Farm, where everything they do is done for their own benefit. Napoleon becomes President of the new Republic of Animal Farm. There are no other candidates. It now appears that Snowball was openly fighting on Jones's side in the Battle of the Cowshed; he had been leading the human forces.

Moses the raven comes back in the summer and talks as before about Sugarcandy Mountain. Boxer's twelfth birthday is approaching, but one day while working at the windmill he falls down from exhaustion. Squealer is sent for and comes to tell them that Napoleon is making arrangements to have Boxer treated in a hospital at Willingdon. After two days Boxer is taken away in a van with lettering on its side which Benjamin reads for them. It reads: 'Alfred Simmonds, Horse Slaughterer and Glue Boiler'. Boxer is being taken to the knacker's. The animals try to warn him, and he attempts to smash his way out of the van, but so weak is he from his devoted work that he lacks the strength to do so. Three days later they are told that Boxer died praising the Rebellion and Comrade Napoleon. Squealer explains the sign on the van by telling them that the veterinary surgeon had bought the van from the knacker, and the old name had not been painted out yet. The pigs hold a banquet in honour of Boxer, to which no one else is invited. Somewhere they have been able to get money to buy whisky for it.

COMMENTARY: The animals believe they are free, and that all they do is done for their own benefit. They fail to see what is so obvious to the reader, that the pigs are no better, and probably even worse, than Jones had been. But then the pigs are experts at controlling memory, and not many can remember the days when Jones owned Animal Farm. What the pigs say happened at the Battle of the Cowshed is now directly contrary to what the reader remembers as having happened there. The animals, with the exception of Benjamin, who says nothing, accept what they are told.

Moses comes back, and tells them again about Sugarcandy Mountain as he had done in Jones's day. Orwell's idea here is that life has become so miserable again that the animals need to believe in some place beyond the sky where there will be peace and plenty. The pigs do not throw him out, in fact they allow him beer every day even though they say his stories are lies. It is convenient for them to have him there, in that the animals will put up with more injustice if they think that when they die they will be in bliss.

The coldness and cruelty of the pigs is nowhere more clearly shown than in their sending the exhausted Boxer to the knacker's to be boiled down for glue. The money they get for him they spend on whisky in his honour.

NOTES AND GLOSSARY:

poultice: a soft mass of meal applied to a wound to ease pain, and quicken healing

tureen: a large dish for soup

Spontaneous Demonstration: a display, or march that has not been planned beforehand

---

Chapter 10

Years pass. Animals die off, but no animal is ever retired. The farm is richer, and has been added to. The windmill has been completed, but it is used for milling corn which is then sold, not for heating the animals' stalls, or for making their work easier. Though the farm is better off the lives of the animals do not change, apart from those of the pigs and dogs, of which there are now a great number. Squealer tells the animals that the pigs are kept busy covering pieces of paper with writing and then burning them in the furnace. Without this, he says, the farm could not function. The animals cannot remember if it was ever better or worse than it is now, apart from Benjamin, who says it never changes. They are aware that theirs is the only farm in all England owned by animals and they are proud of it. They are free, and they are equal, and they look forward to the day when all humans have been expelled from the land, and there will be one united animal England.

One day Squealer takes the sheep off to a quiet place, where he teaches them a new song. They are a week apart from the other animals, then one day soon after their return the animals see, to their astonishment, Squealer walking on his hind legs. Out of the farmhouse come a long line of pigs, all walking on their hind legs, followed by Napoleon, also upright, and looking majestic. He carries a whip in his trotter. In spite of their habit of never complaining, the animals might have made some protest at this reversal of all their ideals but for the fact that at this point the sheep break into their new song: 'Four legs good, two legs *better*'. Clover, now very old, and Benjamin, who hasn't changed much, go to the wall of the big barn where the Seven Commandments are written to find them gone, and the following single Commandment in their place: 'All animals are equal, but some are more equal than others'. After this they learn that the pigs have bought themselves all kinds of human luxuries.

A week later a delegation of humans visit the farm; they make a tour of inspection and are very impressed with what they see. In the evening they go to the farmhouse and the animals hear sounds of laughter coming from it. They creep up and peer in: inside they see Mr Pilkington making a speech complimenting the pigs on how well they have organised the farm. In fact he says that Animal Farm gets more work out of the lower animals for less food than any other farm in the country. There are many features of the farm which he and the other visitors intend to introduce in their own farms immediately. The pigs, he says in a concluding joke, have their lower animals to put up with, while the humans have their lower classes. There is much laughter and cheering at this.

Napoleon replies in a characteristically short speech. He says that the rumours that have gone about saying that the pigs on Animal Farm were trying to stir up Rebellion among the other farms are false. They wish to live in peace with their neighbours. Also, the custom on the farm of addressing one another as 'Comrade' is to be stopped. The name of the farm is to be changed back to Manor Farm, its original name. The animals outside, looking in, think they see something changing in the faces of the pigs: they seem to be melting, shifting. They turn away to go back to their stalls, when a row breaks out in the farmhouse. They turn back and look in again at the violently arguing faces, and they cannot tell the pigs from the human beings. The cause of the argument appears to be that Napoleon and Pilkington both played an ace of spades at the same time.

COMMENTARY: The animals are told that the farm is getting richer all the time (Squealer has the figures to prove it) and yet their lives do not seem to change at all. They are told that one thing is so, when all their experience tells them that it is not. Nevertheless they believe what they are told, rather than what they experience with their senses. The pigs are getting fatter and Napoleon now weighs twenty-four stone.

Benjamin says that hunger and hardship are the 'unalterable law of life'. When the Seven Commandments were first painted on the barn wall it was said that they would in future be the 'unalterable law'. The repeating of the phrase by Benjamin in the last chapter underlines Orwell's bitter irony. The Seven Commandments prove only all too alterable, and by the end of the book not one is left. It would appear that in Orwell's view of things Benjamin has the truth of the matter, that life never really changes, that all systems tend to become tyrannical, that there is a 'vital disease' as he called it once, in the world, which makes a few always impose themselves on the many. It doesn't matter what system is set in motion, Animalism, Socialism, Capitalism, in the end you cannot tell the pigs from the humans. This is Orwell's bleak view at the end of this satire. Do you think this is too dark and pessimistic a conclusion to what he described as 'A Fairy Story'?

The visit of Pilkington and the other humans to Animal Farm at the end reflects the agreements made between Britain, the United States and the Soviet Union, after Hitler had invaded the latter in 1941. Pilkington has Winston Churchill, the British Prime Minister of the war years, behind him. Napoleon and Pilkington end up arguing, because both have the same card up their sleeves. The card is self-interest.

NOTES AND GLOSSARY:

superannuated: retired

co-operative enterprise: an undertaking or experiment where the profits are shared

Part 3

Commentary

Political background

Orwell wrote *Animal Farm* between November 1943 and February 1944, so it was written at the height of the Second World War. He could not find a publisher for the book for some time and it was in fact rejected by Gollancz, Cape, and Faber and Faber, three of London's leading publishers. It was eventually published in August 1945 by Secker and Warburg, but not before Orwell had thought of publishing it at his own expense. T.S. Eliot, who was a director at Faber at the time, sums up the attitude of the publishers unwilling to take the book. Faber, he says, has 'no conviction . . . that this is the right point of view from which to criticise the political situation at the present time'.* Why, in the eyes of three publishers was it not 'the right point of view'?

In 1944 Stalinist Russia was an ally in the war against Germany. The Russian defence of Stalingrad until 1943 against all that Nazi power could pour in to take the city won the admiration of the British public. Also the offensive against Russia had diverted Hitler's attention from England, and she was grateful for that. So, it seemed like ingratitude on Orwell's part to produce a fable in 1944 which attempted to remind the British public that only five years before, in 1939, Stalin had been Hitler's ally. Indeed the Nazi-Soviet pact had helped bring about Hitler's invasion of Poland, and so had been a cause of the war itself. Orwell, like Benjamin in the story, has a clear memory of what happened, but unlike Benjamin, he was not, in 1944, prepared to keep quiet about it.

At this stage it would be best to give a brief outline of the links between modern Russian history and the story of *Animal Farm*. These links are spread out over a long period of time, from 1917, in fact, to 1941 and beyond. Orwell can get away with this telescoping of historical events, and the inevitable simplification that must result, because he is writing neither a history nor a novel. If he were writing a history he would have to go into the details of each event, and show how it came about. If he were writing a novel he would have to show why people behaved the way they did, what combinations of self-

George Orwell: The Critical Heritage, p.20. See Part 5 of these notes for fuller references.

interest and idealism there were, and how they worked out in the clash of temperaments. But he was writing an animal fable, a political fairy story, so the simplifications involved in sweeping through such a long period of time in so short a narrative space are reasonably acceptable.

The main links between the plot of *Animal Farm* and features of modern Russian history can be set down as follows:

(*i*) Old Major's speech corresponds to the thought of Marx, Engels and Lenin. The Seven Commandments correspond to the *Communist Manifesto* of 1848, putting into animal terms the main principles of socialism.

(*ii*) The Rebellion: corresponds to the Bolshevik Rebellion of 1917, led by Lenin.

(*iii*) Battle of the Cowshed: corresponds to the counter-revolutionary war which raged in Russia until 1920. Those Russians fighting the Bolsheviks were helped by Britain and France, just as Jones is aided by neighbouring farmers. Trotsky was in charge of the Red Army, just as in the Battle of the Cowshed Snowball leads the animals.

(*iv*) Napoleon: corresponds to Stalin, who came to power in Russia in 1922. He and Trotsky were opposed almost from the start, just as Napoleon and Snowball are in the story.

(*v*) Confessions and executions in Chapter 7: correspond to the Moscow Trials of the 1930s, when leading Soviet officials confessed publicly to all sorts of offences against the state, and then were shot or imprisoned. The man behind these, it is thought, was Stalin, just as in the story it is quite clear that Napoleon has arranged the confessions, as a warning to the other animals.

(*vi*) The sale of the timber to Frederick of Pinchfield: corresponds to the Nazi-Soviet pact of 1939. Hitler invaded Russia in 1941, just as Frederick attacks the farm and blows up the windmill having deceived Napoleon with false money.

(*vii*) The visit of Pilkington and other neighbours (without Frederick of course): corresponds to the mutual aid agreements between Stalin and Churchill in 1941.

Other links could be detected, but the main point is clear: Orwell is intent on presenting the unpleasant facts (as he sees them) of the Russian Revolution up to his own day. Soon after the book was published relationships between Russia and the Western allies became much cooler; in fact it was the beginning of what is now called the Cold War. In the atmosphere of the Cold War, where public opinion had turned very much against Russia, *Animal Farm* did very well, making Orwell comfortably off for the first time in his life.

Purpose

In an essay called 'Why I Write' written in 1947, Orwell says that his desire has been to make political writing into an art. He starts to write a book, he says, from 'a sense of injustice', not from the idea that he is going to produce a great work of art: 'I write it because there is some lie I want to expose, some fact to which I want to draw attention, and my initial concern is to get a hearing.'*

From the sketch of the political background to *Animal Farm* it will be quite clear that one of the purposes of the book is to expose the lie which (it seemed to Orwell) Stalinist Russia had become. It was supposed to be a Socialist Union of States, but it had become a dictatorship. Not only that, there were socialists in Britain and in the West generally who were so eager to advance the cause that everything the Soviet Union did had to be accepted. The Soviet Union, in fact, damaged the cause of true socialism. In a preface he wrote to *Animal Farm* he says that 'for the past ten years I have been convinced that the destruction of the Soviet myth was essential if we wanted a revival of the socialist movement'.† *Animal Farm* attempts, through a simplification of Soviet history, to clarify in the minds of readers what Orwell felt Russia had become. The clarification is to get people to face the facts of injustice, of brutality, and hopefully to get them to think out for themselves some way in which a true and 'democratic socialism' (in Orwell's phrase) will be brought about.

But Orwell's purpose goes beyond the particular example of the Russian Revolution. In *Animal Farm* he criticises something inherent in all revolutions and he himself was conscious of this. Russia is the immediate example, but the book, Orwell himself said, 'is intended as a satire on dictatorship in general'.‡ The time will come when the details of Russian history that roused Orwell's anger will be forgotten, and *Animal Farm* will be read for its bitter, ironic analysis of the stages all revolutions tend to go through. In *Animal Farm* Orwell is thinking of the French Revolution and of the Spanish Civil War as well as the Bolshevik Rebellion of 1917. After the initial excitement and enthusiasm, when personal interests are *almost* forgotten, Orwell seems to say, the hard facts of life begin to make themselves felt again. To survive one must produce food, and to produce food one must organise. To organise one needs administrators, and they will be among the most intelligent and the most ambitious. Administrative authority gradually becomes power and power becomes tyranny. Orwell sees this process as something that is almost inevitable in

The Collected Essays, Journalism and Letters of George Orwell, I, 28.
†*Collected Essays, Journalism and Letters*, III, 458.
‡MS letter to Leonard Moore, quoted in Alex Zwerdling, *Orwell and the Left*, p.90.

human affairs, Revolution among them. In *Animal Farm* this process works itself out with a logic that is simple and effective.

Was it Orwell's purpose then to present the reader with a view of man's inability to change himself? Such a view would be directly contrary to Orwell's own, very personal brand of socialism, but there is no doubt but that part of him, at least, felt that there was something wrong with human nature and that political systems, because human, had a tendency towards corruption and tyranny. *Animal Farm* is a powerful parable of that tendency.

It would also be possible to take the view that *Animal Farm* confronts its readers with the tendencies towards tyranny in Revolution so that they may be warned. Such things having happened before, they may very well happen again if care is not taken to avoid them, next time. The reader will have to make up his own mind as to whether Orwell was a moral pessimist or a moralistic socialist. It may be that they are the same thing.

Orwell's purposes in writing *Animal Farm* may be summarised:

> (*i*) To expose the 'Soviet myth' as he called it. He saw the mindless acceptance of everything Stalin did in the name of socialism as damaging socialism itself.
> (*ii*) To expose the nature of Revolution itself. The first purpose is the groundwork for the second.
> (*iii*) By doing (*i*) and (*ii*) to get his readers to think about the future of socialism and the future of Western society.

Animal Farm is a work that raises questions not just about political systems, but about human nature itself. Can man change, or is he condemned to a see-saw of systems that all end up the same? Because one of Orwell's deepest purposes was primarily moral, it is not surprising that he chose a form traditionally associated with the moral as a means of achieving his purpose: the animal fable.

The animal fable

As a form the animal fable has a long and distinguished history, going back to *Aesop's Fables*, Chaucer's *Nun's Priest's Tale*, the bestiary poems and fables of the middle ages, down through *La Fontaine's Fables* to the animal stories of Rudyard Kipling, such as the *Jungle Book* and the *Just So Stories*. Indeed, it may be that Kipling's animal stories provided the immediate model for *Animal Farm*.

The animal fable has one great characteristic from which the whole convention of the form derives: that is, that the animals behave in ways that are recognisably like the ways humans behave. In other words the convention humanised the animal figures. Only in that way can it be possible to put animals into a story. As yet we have no way of clearly knowing how animals think, so the animal fable imposes human behaviour and human reactions on the animals. This has four advantages for the moralist:

(1) In the animal fable the writer can simplify human behaviour, without making the reader feel that he is being untrue to human nature. The fox can be associated with the human conception of cunning, but of course real foxes, as distinct from those we find in fables, are not cunning: they are foxes!

(2) Writing of animals as if they were human beings, while all the time conscious that they are not, means that the reader becomes conscious of an element of the ludicrous in the convention. Indeed as Edward M. Thomas has pointed out in his excellent study*, the simplification and the humour are dependent upon one another. The animals in the story are funny because of the obviousness of their motives. The way in which what they are up to is always quite apparent contrasts comically with the complicated way human beings decide on similar courses of action. We cannot see human motivations as clearly as we see the reasons behind what the animals do, so we experience a humourous certainty in our moral attitudes towards them.

The world of the fiction clarifies our moral understanding of the issues involved. This is directly related to what Orwell considered his function as a writer to be: he wanted his readers to understand clearly what he wished to say, to see the issues involved for themselves through his prose. The animal fable has the advantage of simplifying our response and therefore clarifying it. The simplification involves humour.

(3) The fact that the figures in Orwell's fable are animals has the effect of allowing the reader to stand back from the issue: human characters would almost necessarily mean complex involvement with the characters. Here, in the light of Orwell's witty, ironic satire, the reader clearly judges the issues, as *issues*, rather than as the products of the complexity of human action. As readers we naturally become involved with the figures of the fable; indeed Orwell presents them in such a way that we naturally find ourselves taking sides.

(4) The animal fable is usually set in the countryside, naturally, and the rural background of *Animal Farm* is important to its atmosphere. Constantly Orwell reminds us what time of year it is, whether summer, autumn, winter, or spring. The natural backdrop roots the fable in common experience, giving it greater reality, on the one hand, and on the other, greater universality.

*Edward M. Thomas, *George Orwell*, p.74.

Orwell called *Animal Farm* 'a fairy story' but many fairy stories use the conventions of the animal fable in whole or in part. Fairy stories and animal fables relax the laws of everyday experience because such a relaxation is pleasurable, but also because it is often a very useful way of clarifying something about our everyday life. *Animal Farm* is an animal fable where the laws of ordinary life are not in strict operation, and yet, as the tale goes on, we find in it a humorous, and at times disturbingly accurate account of the evil effects of power.

We could sum up the advantages of the animal fable as follows:

(*i*) Through it Orwell can simplify human behaviour, and in this way clarify it. The reader should find examples of how certain animals in *Animal Farm* simplify human behaviour and in so doing clarify it.

(*ii*) Because a simplification of human action involves an exaggeration of certain aspects of it, the animal fable tends to be funny. Find examples of this.

(*iii*) The fable allows the reader to stand back from the issues and judge them as issues.

(*iv*) The rural background of the animal fable gives it realism and universality.

(*v*) It presents a world unlike ours only for us to find that it is very like ours.

Orwell's irony

Irony is one of the most difficult literary terms to define. Simply, it has to do with the writer making the reader (or spectator, in drama) aware of something of which his characters are not aware. This changes the way the reader regards the characters, and sets up a special relationship between him and the writer. The writer and the reader share a better awareness of the nature of what is going on than do the characters in the story. Irony can be used for making the characters seem either comic or pathetic but often both together. For example, at the end of Chapter 2 the animals come back from working on the harvest. Earlier that day the cows had been milked and someone had asked what was to become of the milk. Napoleon had told them not to mind, and had placed himself between the milk and them. When they come back they are puzzled to find the milk gone. The reader here is not the slightest bit puzzled. He knows very well that Napoleon has taken the lot. This is funny, but the innocence and simplicity of the animals have an element of the pathetic in it also. We sense that from now on they are to be fooled again and again.

Another example of Orwell's irony is the changing story of Snowball's part in the Battle of the Cowshed. Soon after he is expelled Squealer prophesies to the animals that in time it will appear that Snowball's part in the Battle was 'much exaggerated'.* Later on he tells them that Snowball had been in league with Jones all the time, and that in fact he had attempted to get them defeated at the Battle (p.69). Eventually they are told that he had 'actually been the leader of the human forces, and had charged into battle with the words "Long live Humanity!" on his lips' (p.99).

Unlike the animals, the reader has a very clear recollection of what happened at the Cowshed. Snowball had bravely led the attack that won the Battle, and had been wounded in the back by Jones. The reader remembers this, but the animals cannot. The irony here is comic (their blind acceptance of what they are told by the disgusting Squealer is ridiculous), but it is also pathetic; pathetic because we know they have lost all sense of the objective truth of what happened, and so are easy prey to the likes of Napoleon.

There is a moral or satiric overtone to this irony as well. Orwell seems to be saying to his reader: 'look at these animals; is not the way they are duped ridiculous? Are you sure you yourself are not being duped by someone the equivalent of Napoleon?' So the irony can be said to have three functions: (1) comic, (2) pathetic, and (3) moral, or satiric. The reader should make a list of examples of Orwell's use of irony. If he does he will see that almost every episode in the book has its ironic qualities and that the three different aspects of irony listed above are entirely inseparable in any given example.

As an example we may take the episode in Chapter 3 where Snowball explains to the birds that wings are not wings but legs, so that they can think of themselves as four-legged creatures, and so fit the maxim of Animalism: 'Four legs good, two legs bad':

'A bird's wing, comrades', he said, 'is an organ of propulsion and not of manipulation. It should therefore be regarded as a leg. The distinguishing mark of Man is the *hand*, the instrument with which he does all his mischief.'
The birds did not understand Snowball's long words, but they accepted his explanation (p.31).

Snowball's long-winded attempt to make a leg out of a wing is, of course, comic, as are the long words he uses in his frantic attempt to do the impossible. The unthinking acceptance by the birds of a proof that is not a proof at all is also absurd and funny, but there is an element of

Animal Farm, p.50. References throughout are to the Penguin edition. Further references are given after quotations in the text.

the pathetic here also. Their innocence and stupidity make them prey to such absurdities. Furthermore, when we think that later on the pigs can get the animals to accept anything they want them to accept then the moral and satiric overtones of this passage become clear. A leg is a leg and not a wing, but once the animals can be convinced that what they thought was so is no longer so, then later on facts themselves can be changed to fit in with new developments. Ideology can become thought-control.

Structure

There are different ways of looking at structures of plays, novels or poems. One of the less fruitful ways is to think of structure as a kind of scaffolding on which the characters, themes, ironies or whatever, can be hung. This is to think of structure as some kind of support system, almost as if it were not a living part of the whole work. The word 'living' may help us here, because one of the more useful ways of looking at the structure is to consider it in something like the way we consider the structures of living things. If we think of structure in something like the way we think of bones, tissues, sinews, arteries and ligaments binding the arm of a man together, making it something forceful, alert, and effective, then we are looking at structure in a more helpful way. The sort of questions we should ask about the structure of a work of art are: what draws it together? what gives it force? what makes it effective?

One of the things which draws *Animal Farm* together, that helps to give it force, that makes it effective, is its irony. The ironic structure of the book has two main centres of force, and they both have to do with the wiping out of the memories of the animals. One is the manipulation of their attitudes towards Snowball, the erasing of what they thought they knew of him. And the other has to do with the altering of the Seven Commandments throughout the story. In both cases the reader is well aware of the facts, as the animals were at first. He knows, for example, that Snowball was quite well-intentioned, that he was clever, and that he fought bravely at the Battle of the Cowshed. He also knows what the Seven Commandments said. They were listed clearly and unambiguously in the text, just as they were listed on the wall of the barn. The reader remembers, the animals are not sure. They *think* they remember that Snowball fought bravely, they *think* that the Seven Commandments said something very clear about animals never killing each other, but all of them (apart from Benjamin) are a little uncertain about what they recollect. Napoleon takes advantage of their uncertainty to control them. The extent of his control widens as the book goes on, the irony becomes less comic, more pathetic, the moral and satiric overtones become stronger. Also, the reader's anger mounts at the cruel and heartless way in which Napoleon takes advantage of the gullibility of the animals, until he comes to the episode where Boxer is carted off to the knacker's, when he is sickened by the injustice and cruelty. In the last chapter the irony becomes thoroughly dark indeed. The pigs start walking on their hind legs and in the end are indistinguishable from humans. All that the animals hoped for has been undone. What makes the irony savage in this last chapter is that the animals still cannot understand. They do not realise what is being inflicted on them. They are victims of merciless calculation.

The figures in the fable

For obvious reasons it would be inappropriate to call the figures in Orwell's animal fable characters, despite the fact that he does, with certain of the animals, give them fairly definite characteristics. But they are not human, they are a simplification of the human, so it is more appropriate to speak of them as figures in the fable, and to discuss Orwell's handling of them. His handling of the figures, the way he gets us to sympathise with certain of them and to loathe certain others makes his purpose clearer, and makes the book itself more forceful and effective. This is why the figures are being discussed in the section on structure, because the handling of the figures structures our emotional responses to the story, gets us to take sides and so helps Orwell to achieve his purpose.

The figures divide into two groups: the pigs and the dogs on the one side, and the rest of the animals on the other. Even the dogs do not entirely belong with the pigs, because Napoleon has trained them specially for his cruel purposes, taking them away from their mothers Jessie and Bluebell as soon as they are born. They have been conditioned (in the modern phrase) to hate, and to give fierce, unthinking loyalty to the pigs.

The pigs

The first pig we are introduced to is Old Major, the prize Middle White boar. He is kindly and sympathetic, and has a wise and benevolent appearance' (p.6). When he speaks in the old barn, to pass on to the other animals the wisdom he has learnt from life, there is an atmosphere of warmth and friendship. When the two cart-horses, Boxer and Clover, come in, they step carefully in case they will hurt the smaller creatures in the straw, and Clover makes a sort of wall with her foreleg for a brood of ducklings which have lost their mother. In this atmosphere of warm kindness Old Major tells them that Man is the great enemy, that he is 'the only creature that consumes without providing' (p.9). All animals must be comrades, he says, and the time will come when Man will be gone forever from England's fields. He gives them the song 'Beasts of England'. Soon after this Old Major dies.

The two most important pigs in the fable are Napoleon and Snowball. Snowball is more lively than Napoleon, but Napoleon is deep, does not say much and tends to get his own way. These two are boars, the rest of the pigs on the farm are porkers. One of the porkers, Squealer, plays an important part in the book. He is very good at convincing others. These three develop the system of Animalism from Old Major's ideas.

In the first days of the Rebellion, Snowball and Napoleon work fairly well together, although they have very different ideas about policy. Snowball is a good organiser, is intelligent, and wants to educate the other animals up to the level of the pigs. Napoleon, however, thinks that it is much more important to educate the young, and so takes away Jessie's and Bluebell's puppies to train them up to his purposes. Snowball thinks of others in an idealistic way, while already Napoleon is thinking of himself and planning for the future. For all Snowball's idealism, though, he does not protest when Napoleon decides that the milk and the apples are reserved exclusively for the pigs. Snowball is brave, however, and in the Battle of the Cowshed he fights honourably (while Napoleon is noticeably absent) and is wounded.

Snowball is interested in modernisation, and in improving facilities for the animals on the farm; it is with this in mind that he wishes to build a windmill. A windmill, though it will be hard work to build, will provide electric light and hot and cold water, and do a good deal of the work on the farm. Napoleon violently disagrees. The great need of the moment is, according to him, to increase food production; they will starve to death if they waste time attempting to build a windmill. Another disagreement they have is over the principles of Revolution: Snowball feels they should stir up discontent on other farms, and so provoke extensive Rebellion. Napoleon, on the other hand, feels that defence is the most important priority; that fire-arms should be got and that they should train themselves in the use of them. Eventually their conflict comes to a head and Snowball is run off the farm by Napoleon's dogs, just when it looks as if Snowball is going to win the animals over to his way of thinking. After he has been run off Snowball is blamed for anything that goes wrong.

With Snowball gone Napoleon has a free hand; straightaway it begins to be apparent to the reader that what he wants is complete power and control. He can get the animals to think exactly what he wants them to think through Squealer's persuasiveness and through the fierceness of his dogs.

Orwell presents Napoleon to us in ways that are, at first, amusing as, for example, in the scene where he shows his pretended disdain at Snowball's plans for the windmill by lifting his leg and urinating on the chalked floor. But there are two scenes where Napoleon's cruelty and cold violence are shown in all their horror: the scene of the trials and the episode where Boxer is brought to the knacker's. The veil of mockery is drawn aside. In these episodes, humour is absent, the stark reality of Napoleon's hunger for power, and the cruelty and death it involves are presented. Orwell reminds us of the 'heavy' stink of blood, and associates that smell with Napoleon:

> And so the tale of confessions and executions went on, until there was a pile of corpses lying before Napoleon's feet and the air was heavy with the smell of blood, which had been unknown there since the expulsion of Jones (p.74).

The discussion of Napoleon's treatment of Boxer is held over until we come to deal with Boxer's own place in the fable.

As the tale goes on Napoleon becomes more and more corrupt, more and more merciless, and one by one the original Commandments are altered to fit in with what he wishes to do. For all his cleverness, though, he is fooled by Frederick of Pinchfield who gets the timber out of him, pays him in false money, then attacks the farm, and blows up the windmill.

He likes his comfort, so he moves into the house, and develops a taste for whisky. During his first drunken binge he is seen to totter out of the house wearing an old hat of Jones's, gallop around the yard a few times, then disappear again. Despite his increasing cruelty, Orwell manages to keep him ludicrous up to the very end.

By the end of the story he has put on immense weight, has a huge number of children, whom he keeps separate from the other animals, and eventually starts wearing human clothes and walking on his hind legs, as all the other pigs do. At last the pigs are indistinguishable from human beings.

Napoleon is a simple figure. Orwell makes no attempt to give reasons as to why he comes to act the way he does. If Napoleon were a human character in a novel, if this were a *historical* novel about a historical figure Orwell would have had to make Napoleon convincing in human terms. But he is not human, and this is not a novel. It is an animal fable and Orwell presents the figure of Napoleon in ways that make us both see clearly and despise what he stands for. He is simplified for the sake of clarity. He lends force to Orwell's political message, that power tends to corrupt, by allowing the reader to fix his disgust at cruelty, torture and violence on one leading character. The way Orwell presents the figure is structural, in that the figure of Napoleon clarifies his political intent for the reader. There is no doubt about the way the reader feels towards Napoleon, but Orwell's handling of him is all the more effective for combining humour with the disgust.

We could sum up the main points to make about Napoleon as follows:

(*i*) He is cunning and deep. He does not say much, but acts suddenly and with force. (*ii*) He wants power for the sake of power. Contrast this with Snowball. (*iii*) He is ruthless, but he is also amusing. He rouses our disgust and for that reason we are glad to find him funny. Why?

The other animals

The primary objective of the tale is that we should loathe Napoleon for what he stands for. The other animals are used to intensify our disgust, or else to add colour and life to the tale by the addition of farmyard detail. The most significant of the other animals is undoubtedly the cart-horse Boxer, and in his handling of him Orwell shows great expertise in controlling the reader's reactions and sympathies and in turning them against what he hates.

Throughout the book Boxer is a very sympathetic figure. Honest and hardworking, he is devoted to the cause in a simple-minded way, although his understanding of the principles of Animalism is very limited. He is strong and stands nearly eighteen hands high, and is much respected by the other animals. He has two phrases which for him solve all problems, one, 'I shall work harder', and later on, despite the fact that Napoleon's rule is becoming tyrannical, 'Napoleon is always right'. At one point he does question Squealer, when he, in his persuasive way, is convincing the animals that Snowball was trying to betray them in the Battle of the Cowshed. Boxer at first cannot take this; he remembers the wound Snowball received along his back from Jones's gun. Squealer explains this by saying that it had been arranged for Snowball to be wounded; it had all been part of Jones's plan. Boxer's confused memory of what actually happened makes him 'a little uneasy' (p.71), but when Squealer announces, very slowly, that Napoleon 'categorically' states that Snowball was Jones's agent from the start then the honest cart-horse accepts the absurdity without question.

Orwell, through the figure of Boxer, is presenting a simple good-nature, which wishes to do good, and which believes in the Rebellion. So loyal is Boxer that he is prepared to sacrifice his memory of facts, blurred as it is. Nevertheless, so little is he respected, and so fierce is the hatred the pigs have for even the slightest questioning of their law that, when Napoleon's confessions and trials begin, Boxer is among the first the dogs attack. With his great strength he has no difficulty in controlling them: he just simply, almost carelessly 'put out his great hoof, caught a dog in mid-air, and pinned him to the ground' (p.72). At a word from Napoleon he lets the dog go, but still he doesn't realise he is a target. This show of power pleases us as readers, in that we like to think of physical strength being allied to good nature, simple though that good nature may be. Boxer has our sympathy because he gives his strength selflessly for what he believes, whereas Napoleon gives nothing, believes in nothing (except pigs) and never actually works. Boxer exhausts himself for the cause. Every time the animals have to start re-building the windmill he throws himself into the task without a word of complaint, getting up first half an hour, then three quarters of an hour before everybody else.

At last his great strength gives out, and when it does his goodness is unprotected. One day he is found lying between the shafts of his cart, exhausted. He is brought back to the farm and put in his stall. The pigs have decided that he is to be sent to a vet in Willingdon for special treatment, or at least that is what they tell the other animals. They are, of course, going to send him to the knacker's, to be killed and then boiled down into glue. Warned by Benjamin the donkey (his close, silent friend throughout the book), and by Clover, he tries to kick his way out of the van, but he has given all his energy to the pigs and now has none left to save himself.

This is the most moving scene in the book. Orwell has created in the reader a warm, simple attachment to the powerful, devoted work-horse. Though the reader does not become involved with Boxer in the complex way a reader shares the life of an Emma (see Jane Austen's *Emma*) or a Leopold Bloom (see James Joyce's *Ulysses*) nevertheless he does become involved with him in a sentimental and emotional way, that is no less deep for being simple. Indeed our feelings here as readers are so 'simple, deep and uninhibited' that, as Edward M. Thomas has said movingly, 'we weep for the terrible pity of it like children who meet injustice for the first time'.*

Despite Boxer's devotion to the cause he is treated with cruel injustice by Napoleon and this injustice is calculated to excite in the reader a disgust and hatred for what Napoleon embodies, and Napoleon embodies the injustices of dictatorship. So the figure of
*Thomas, p.76.

Boxer and the sentimental attachment Orwell makes the reader feel
for him clarify the reader's hatred for injustice, and that is the effect
Orwell seeks. Boxer has an important part to play in the structure of
the political fable Orwell has constructed.

When the fat, revolting Squealer comes out and explains to the
animals that the knacker's van was not the knacker's van the reader
sees quite clearly what he is up to if the animals (apart from Benjamin)
do not. (At this point the reader may be reminded of the wing that is
not a wing.) Orwell has controlled the reader's sympathies for Boxer
so well that the reader finds himself hating the pigs *for* the animals,
seeing that the animals cannot hate for themselves. What was the
source of ironic comedy, the fact that the reader knows very well what
the pigs are up to if the animals do not, is now the source of the
reader's anger, an anger Orwell has carefully constructed. Clearly,
Orwell involves his reader's sympathies in order to make his point.

We could sum up the main points to be made about Boxer as
follows:

(*i*) Orwell rouses the reader's sympathies for Boxer by making him
strong, honest, hardworking, loyal and devoted to the cause of
Animalism. He is not very clever and accepts everything the
pigs think fit to tell him.

(*ii*) By having the pigs dispose of him in the cruel way they do,
Orwell converts the reader's affection for Boxer into anger
against the pigs, and the injustice they represent.

(*iii*) For these reasons Boxer is vital to the structure of sympathies
in the fable.

Of the other horses, Clover is an affectionate, motherly mare who tries
to warn Boxer throughout the book against working too hard. Mollie,
the 'foolish, pretty white mare' (p.7), likes sugar lumps and loves to
wear brightly coloured ribbons. When the Rebellion comes it does not
really suit her. She dislikes hard work and often shirks. Eventually
she defects (goes over to the humans) and is seen by the pigeons (who
act as a communications service with the outside world) between the
shafts of a small cart 'painted red and black' (p.42), outside a public-
house in the village.

Benjamin the donkey is an odd figure. He is the oldest animal on
the farm. He says very little and if he does say something it is usually
cynical. He never laughs, because, he maintains, there is nothing to
laugh at. He is, however, completely devoted to Boxer, and they spend
long hours together in the paddock on Sundays, never speaking. He is
never surprised by anything and when the Rebellion comes he is not
impressed. It is as if he has seen it all before. The animals ask him in
the beginning if he is not pleased now that Jones is gone and his reply

is: 'Donkeys live a long time. None of you has ever seen a dead donkey' (p.27), which probably means that he, like all donkeys, is interested in survival, so he is going to keep his mouth shut.

Alone among the animals Benjamin is well aware of what the pigs are up to, but he keeps silent. It is he who tells the animals that Alfred Simmonds the knacker is taking Boxer away, and it is he who reads out the notice along the side of the van, a notice none of them can read. It is he, too, who reads out to Clover the final Commandment on the barn wall: 'All animals are equal but some animals are more equal than others' (p.114). He understands all that happens, but remains passive in order to survive. Thomas suggests that Benjamin is the closest we get to a representative of Orwell in the book.*

There are a number of even lesser figures among the animals. There is Muriel the goat, slightly more intelligent than the others, apart from Benjamin and the pigs; and there is Moses the raven. Moses is an interesting figure. While Jones is still owner he flies about the farm, telling the animals of a place called 'Sugarcandy Mountain', which is a kind of animal heaven. The idea of this, Orwell implies, makes their joyless lives under Jones more acceptable and this is why Jones encourages him. When the Rebellion comes Moses leaves, presumably because now that the animals have something to live for they no longer need a compensation in the after life. When the first ideals of the Rebellion are forgotten, and when Napoleon has become at least as great a tyrant as Jones, Moses returns. Once again, Orwell implies, their lives now being miserable again, they need the consolation of religion once more. When he returns the pigs tolerate Moses, and even encourage him by giving him a ration of their precious beer.

The sheep are the most infuriating group of animals. Not one of them has an identity. They are simply a stupid mass, and can be got to think or do anything. They like the phrase that Snowball concocts as a simplification of the principles of Animalism: 'Four legs good: two legs bad', and blare it out at every opportunity. Stupid as they are they seem to have a sixth sense for moments that are difficult for the pigs, and at these times they drown out all questions by mindless bleating of their inane phrase. This they do for example when Napoleon, having got rid of Snowball, bans the Sunday discussion meetings. Through getting us, as readers, irritated with the sheep, Orwell is getting us irritated with what the sheep represent: mindless, stupid acceptance of power. Their very mindlessness helps keep Napoleon in control. Indeed when Squealer teaches them a completely opposite phrase: 'Four legs good, two legs *better*', to fit in with the fact that the pigs now find it better to walk on two, they take to that just as easily.

Pigeons and other birds act as communicators with animals outside,

*Thomas, p.77.

and as sources of information about the world of the humans. The rats continue to give trouble, despite the ideals of the Rebellion.

There are some humans in the story but they play a small part, and are given very simple characterisation, to fit in with the simplicity of the moral fable. Jones, the original owner of Animal Farm, is a lazy, careless farmer. He has failed to make the most out of what he owns and has responsibility for. He is fond of drink (a fondness which, ironically, the pigs themselves develop as their power increases). For a time Jones stays in the village spreading bad reports about the way things are going on the farm, then he makes an attempt to take it back but is defeated at the Battle of the Cowshed. Eventually he leaves and dies in a home for alcoholics in another part of the country.

The two neighbouring farmers, Pilkington and Frederick, are mainly here for the historical significance of the tale. They stand for England and Germany respectively, and the complicated to-ing and fro-ing in Napoleon's relationship with them represents the uncertain nature of Russia's relations with England and Germany from 1917 to 1943. Pilkington's farm, Foxwood, is an easygoing, careless sort of place, the sort of place Orwell thought that England was, but that he felt it could no longer afford to be. Frederick is shrewd and tough but keeps a well-organised farm. Frederick outwits Napoleon, for all Napoleon's cunning, paying him in forged money for the timber he wants. Other human characters are Mr Whymper, Napoleon's agent with the outer world, who does well out of Animal Farm, and Mrs Jones, who makes a fleeting appearance as she escapes out of the back door.

The plot

There are seven main turning-points in the plot:

(*i*) The Rebellion itself.
(*ii*) The Battle of the Cowshed.
(*iii*) The expulsion of Snowball.
(*iv*) The mock confessions and mock trials of Napoleon.
(*v*) The Battle of the Windmill.
(*vi*) The betrayal of Boxer.
(*vii*) The party at the end.

Each one of these directs the reader's sympathies in different ways. The reader should try to decide how it is so directed at each point and to what purpose.

Style

In *Animal Farm* Orwell uses a simple straightforward prose style, a style that is entirely appropriate to the convention of the animal fable itself, and to the purpose Orwell had in mind when writing it. 'Good prose is like a window-pane', Orwell said.* He felt strongly that prose should be functional and effective, should convey clearly what the writer wishes to say, and should not get in the way of the reader's understanding. Looked at in this way, clarity of style has political overtones, in that, if a prose writer feels that what he has to say is a matter of some urgency then he has a responsibility to make his language a clear, transparent medium which the reader may look through, and see the issues clearly.

In *Animal Farm* Orwell wants to tell a story which will make quite clear the dangers of Socialist Revolution, how easily it may give way to Fascist dictatorship, and in so doing make clear a danger in all Revolution. He makes his style as plain as possible so that his message may be clear. He chooses simple words and uncomplicated phrases in his narration. Sometimes he complicates the dialogue, by making the pigs speak a jargon. By contrast to the simple style of the narration Snowball's absurd jargon, where a wing becomes 'an organ of propulsion', is ludicrous. Again the change of style is deliberately chosen to make Snowball's jargon, and the jargon of Marxist analysis which it deliberately makes fun of, look completely unreal. Style and purpose are closely knit in *Animal Farm*.

Climax

The last chapter of *Animal Farm*, where the climax comes, is separated from the other events of the book by a considerable gap in time. The chapter opens like this: 'Years passed. The seasons came and went, the short animal lives went by' (p.108). Up to now the tale has kept to a fairly tight time flow. The first nine chapters give us the history of Animal Farm in its first four years. Between Chapters 9 and 10 years pass.

Orwell has a perfectly good reason for this. In Chapter 9 we had the very moving death of Boxer. It is now right, from the narrative point of view, that Orwell should give a sense of time passing. It gives the reader a sense of distance from the action, seeing that he has been so involved in it in Chapter 9 with the death of Boxer. Furthermore, if Orwell had continued without a gap in time he might have been led back into the comic mode, and that would have been all wrong after Boxer's death. (Why?) Now he goes straight into his startling climax.

An odd thing happens here, in view of the convention of the animal

*Collected Essays, Journalism and Letters, I, 30.

fable which Orwell has been using all along. Pigs do not talk, nor horses, donkeys, or goats, but we have accepted that they do in the tale. They do not form political systems either, but it is necessary that we accept the fable that they do if Orwell is to achieve his political and artistic purpose. But now, at the climax of the tale, Orwell turns the convention on its head. The pigs start walking on their hind legs, and at the end the animals looking through the window at the party of humans and pigs gathered inside the house cannot tell the difference. Why does Orwell turn the convention upside down? Mainly in order to satisfy his political purposes:

(i) Orwell wants to show that for the animals on Animal Farm there is now no difference between the rule of Jones at the beginning and pig rule.

(ii) To show that power can alter nature itself. The pigs have forsaken their animal natures and are becoming human.

(iii) To remind us that though we have been accepting the convention of the animal fable the moral of the fable has to do with us as human beings. It all comes back to human nature, even the fable.

As well as effectively underlining his political purpose the change is also acceptable artistically, in that the pigs throughout the tale have gradually become more and more human. They move into the house, engage in trade, get a taste for whisky, and take out subscriptions to *John Bull*, an English periodical popular in the 1940s. The irony, of course, is that in becoming more human they become more like real animals all the time, and more unlike the other animals on Animal Farm, who retain many human traits.

How would the reader judge this climax? Would he say it is pessimistic or optimistic? Much opinion would hold that the climax is a reflection of Orwell's increasingly pessimistic view of human nature; that the story leaves us with an overwhelming sense of the futility of all Revolution, of all change. Orwell is simplifying the issues involved here, and simplification must run to extremes, nevertheless, it is probably fair to say that the climax of the book leaves us with a sense of the futility of man's effort to improve his lot. It is almost as if Orwell sees man as being condemned by some basic flaw in his nature, the flaw that Catholics would call original sin, what Orwell called 'some kind of mental disease which must be diagnosed before it can be cured'.*

Other viewpoints are possible: Raymond Williams says that the climax allows the animals *outside* to see clearly that now there is no difference between pigs and humans. They have a clear sight of the

*Collected Essays, Journalism and Letters, IV, 288–9.

enemy. Next time, in the next Rebellion, they may know better. Mr Williams calls this a 'potentially liberating discovery' for the animals outside.* Professor Alex Zwerdling maintains that if Orwell has a positive point of view in *Animal Farm* it is the hope that socialists who believe in Revolution will face the unpleasant truths he presents about tendencies in human nature that idealists like to forget.†

The reader will of course have to make up his own mind about the interpretation of the climax, but he would do well to consider the value of the various viewpoints expressed above in the light of his own feelings about the tale.

*Raymond Williams, *Orwell*, p.74.
†Zwerdling, p.93.

Part 4

Hints for study

Points for detailed study

Theme

One aspect of *Animal Farm* that all students should consider carefully is its theme. The theme of the book is closely related to its purpose. Orwell's purpose in writing *Animal Farm* was to show, as effectively as possible, that political idealism can turn sour, as he felt it had done in Russia after the 1917 Rebellion. His theme then is basically that political ideals collapse, to give way to tyranny. The fact that he called the main figure of the book Napoleon (the name of the great leader of post-Revolutionary France) indicates that he was thinking not just of modern Russia but of a basic tendency in human nature.

Purpose then, and theme (which is the carrying out of the purpose), are central and can be referred to in almost any question on the book, once the reader understands what they are and how they work. For example, if the reader comes upon a question on Orwell's style, it would be very possible to refer to purpose and theme, showing how Orwell's simplicity in style is used deliberately to achieve the purpose of the book, to convey the theme. Orwell wants us to understand his purpose clearly, wants us to make no mistake about his theme, so his style remains as transparent as a window-pane. Except of course when he makes it deliberately obscure, in Snowball's explanations, in order to underline his theme. How do you think this obscurity underlines the theme?

A discussion of the handling of the different figures in the fable can also be referred to the theme. The contrast between Snowball and Napoleon develops certain aspects of the theme. What aspects are these?

Setting

Animal Farm is set in rural England, and Orwell effectively sketches the natural background for the reader. All through the book we are reminded of the detail of the countryside and the movement of the seasons. How does this contribute to the tale?

(a) The details of rural life, the five-barred gate, the hedges, the little knoll where the windmill is built – all these root the tale for us in a real life we know or can imagine. The reader should find examples and consider them.

(b) The movement of the seasons, and the recurring cycles of nature give the tale a *generalised* quality, which helps to make it into a kind of universal parable. The reader should find examples and consider them.

(c) Another aspect of the setting is Orwell's use of details which are strictly speaking unnecessary. Old Major, for example, is a 'Middle White boar'. Napoleon likes to drink his beer from a 'Crown Derby soup tureen', and by the end of the fable he is 'a mature boar of twenty-four stone'. Many examples can be found.

Conflict

Conflict operates on a number of levels throughout *Animal Farm*. Firstly there is the obvious conflict between Jones and the animals, which stands, in the tale, for the conflict between exploiter and the exploited, upper class and lower class. Jones, is defeated but a second conflict arises among the animals, that between Snowball and Napoleon. See the discussion of Orwell's handling of the pigs in the Commentary, for some further points on this conflict. Then there is the conflict between Animal Farm and the outside world, the shifting relationships with Pilkington and Frederick, and the eventual open conflict with the latter. Also, more subtly, there is the conflict which the animals themselves occasionally feel in their minds, when what the pigs tell them to be true is not what they think they remember. All these conflicts are used by Orwell to point his moral, to drive his purpose home. How?

The animal fable

Orwell's adaptation of the convention of the animal fable is fundamental to almost any discussion of the book as a whole. The reader will probably find himself referring to it in almost every context. Through it he achieves his purpose.

Character

It is unlikely that a reader will be asked to discuss characterisation in this book, since there are only a handful of humans, who are very faintly sketched. If a reader is asked to deal with character he may take it he is being asked to discuss the animal figures.

Useful quotations

Old Major's principles: 'All men are enemies. All animals are comrades' (p.11). Of man, Old Major says: 'We must not come to resemble him.' By the end of the tale the pigs have forgotten these principles. They not only resemble man, they become him.

Examples of unnecessary details introduced to give vividness: The following is a description of the inside of the house after the animals take it over: 'the beds with their feather mattresses, the looking-glasses, the horsehair sofa, the Brussels carpet, the lithograph of Queen Victoria over the drawing-room mantelpiece' (p.21).

Napoleon's dogs keep close to him: 'It was noticed that they wagged their tails to him in the same way as the other dogs had been used to do to Mr Jones' (p.48). This indicates early on that Napoleon is going to be another, and perhaps even worse, Mr Jones.

Squealer, in explaining why Napoleon had seemed to be opposed to the Windmill in order to get Snowball out, calls this 'tactics': 'He repeated a number of times, "Tactics, comrades, tactics!" skipping round and whisking his tail with a merry laugh' (p.52). The animals do not understand the word 'tactics'. Here Squealer is using language to blind rather than to reveal, a technique of which dictatorship, according to Orwell, is fond.

'I will work harder', and 'Napoleon is always right': Boxer's explanations for everything.

The animals are told that Snowball is responsible for all ills that befall the farm. They find him everywhere, as if he were 'some kind of invisible influence, pervading the air about them and menacing them with all kinds of dangers' (p.69). This shows that Napoleon has erected a fear of Snowball out of nothing, and that this fear helps him keep the animals subject.

The horrifying cruelty of Napoleon's rule: 'There was a pile of corpses lying before Napoleon's feet and the air was heavy with the smell of blood' (p.74).

Squealer comes and reads out figures to the animals, proving that the farm is producing sometimes as much as five times the amount of food as in the days before the Rebellion, yet the animals still go hungry: 'All the same, there were days when they felt they would sooner have less figures and more food' (p.79).

The hypocrisy of the pigs, and their perverting of the principles of Animalism: 'A too rigid equality in rations, Squealer explained, would have been contrary to the principles of Animalism' (p.95).

Napoleon, walking on his hind legs, in all his tyrannical majesty: 'There was a tremendous baying of dogs and a shrill crowing from the black cockerel, and out came Napoleon himself, majestically upright, casting haughty glances from side to side, and with his dogs gambolling round him. He carried a whip in his trotter' (p.113).

The final transformation: 'Twelve voices were shouting in anger, and they were all alike. No question, now, what had happened to the faces of the pigs. The creatures outside looked from pig to man, and from man to pig, and from pig to man again; but already it was impossible to say which was which' (p.120).

Arrangement of material

In answering questions on *Animal Farm* the reader should bear the following points in mind:

- (*i*) That Orwell had a political purpose in writing it, and that this determines the way he presents his story.
- (*ii*) That he uses the convention of the animal fable because it simplifies and therefore clarifies the issues he wishes to present.
- (*iii*) That the irony of the fable is comic, pathetic and moral.
- (*iv*) That the tale darkens towards its close, the irony becoming more satiric, more moral.
- (*v*) That the fable is based on modern Russian history, but has general application.

So when considering how to answer a question try to keep Orwell's purpose in mind and the different ways he achieves it: fable, handling of the figures, and so on. If the reader does this then the answer he will produce will be *central* to Orwell's concern. It would probably be a mistake to spend too much time on the precise political background, on the Nazi-Soviet pact of 1939, for example, unless asked specifically to deal with these aspects. If such a question arises it will be easy: facts are facts. But it is more likely that the questions the reader will encounter will have to do with purpose, theme (they are closely related), use of the fable, handling of figures (they may be called characters), irony or style. All of these dovetail one into the other, which may be an advantage in some cases, but in others it will be a disadvantage. For example, if the question were one on style, the discussion would have to be fairly practical and the reader would need to stop himself getting too involved in theoretical discussions. However, most of the time the reader will find that the difficult aspects of the book throw light on each other, and he will be able to draw them together in his answers. This is because Orwell has made the different aspects of the fable serve his purpose so well.

Specimen questions

(1) '*Animal Farm* was the first book in which I tried, with full consciousness of what I was doing, to fuse political purpose and artistic purpose into one whole.' (George Orwell, 'Why I Write') Discuss.

(2) 'I write . . . because there is some lie that I want to expose, . . . and my initial concern is to get a hearing.' ('Why I Write') What lie or lies does Orwell wish to expose in *Animal Farm*? How does he make sure he gets a hearing?

(3) Trace the growth of the power of the pigs in *Animal Farm*. What lessons does Orwell wish us to draw from this?

(4) Compare the figures of Snowball and Napoleon. What part does each play in the achievement of Orwell's purpose?

(5) Examine the role of Squealer in the development of the new system of control on *Animal Farm*.

(6) Why did Orwell locate his satire on political power on a farm in the English countryside?

(7) Examine the role of the sheep in *Animal Farm*.

(8) In your view is *Animal Farm* an optimistic or a pessimistic book?

(9) How does Orwell contrive to involve us in a story which is about animals?

(10) Examine the humour of *Animal Farm*. Is it all of the same kind throughout?

(11) Discuss Orwell's use of irony in *Animal Farm*.

Suggested model answer

(1) '*Animal Farm* was the first book in which I tried, with full consciousness of what I was doing, to fuse political purpose and artistic purpose into one whole.' (George Orwell, 'Why I Write') Discuss.

Orwell's political purpose in *Animal Farm* was threefold: he wished (*i*) to expose the faults which he saw as being inherent in revolutionary socialism, (*ii*) to warn his readers of a tendency towards corruption in all Revolutions, as he saw them, and (*iii*) to remind the British public of the atrocities of Stalinist Russia in the 1930s. At the time of writing (1943–4) Britain was inclined to forget what had happened in Russia in the 1930s because Stalin was now an ally in the war against Germany. Only four years before, however, he had been an enemy, and Orwell did not want his readers to be like the sheep in the book, blandly accepting everything they are told, not remembering what is inconvenient. As a writer Orwell considered it his duty to face up to and present unpleasant facts in as clear a way as possible. The parable of *Animal Farm* is based on Russian history from 1917 to the time of writing, but his theme is also all Revolutions. Napoleon is named after Napoleon Bonaparte, the great leader of post-Revolutionary France.

If these were his purposes, exposing the corrupt tendencies in Revolution, and reminding the public of what they might find it more convenient to forget, why then did he not write a pamphlet, clearly outlining his ideas? As a writer he wanted to convey his political message as forcefully as possible and in doing so he adopted an oblique approach by pretending that his tale was about a farm where a Rebellion takes place. He chose the old form of the animal fable. In doing this, in writing about politics while pretending to be writing about something entirely different, he was following the example of Swift in *Gulliver's Travels*, one of his favourite books. Orwell's pretence and Swift's are very thin; every reader knows that more is going on than meets the eye, but the pretence gives the writer greater freedom.

The freedom the pretence gives in *Animal Farm* is the freedom to simplify, which a convention allows. The story is set on a farm, the characters are animals, who behave in ways comparable to humans, but who are not human. Not being human, Orwell does not have to bother about making them believable. If Napoleon were a human character Orwell could not make him as completely unpleasant as he does. Because Napoleon is a pig Orwell can exaggerate his unpleasantness, his cruelty and greed and in this way underline and clarify the point he is trying to make: that power, even 'Animalist' power, tends to corrupt. In exaggerating the unpleasantness and greed of Napoleon, Orwell is not only clarifying his political point, he is also being funny. But the pigs are funny only up to a certain point. When they begin to kill, when we get the 'heavy' stink of blood in our noses, then they begin to cease being funny and become horrifying. Strangely, they are even more horrifying for having been funny.

In another way the animal fable helps Orwell achieve his political purpose. It involves our feelings in ways that are deep and simple. We grow attached to Boxer, for example, in the simple way we do grow attached to animals. When he is treated cruelly by the pigs Orwell turns our affection for Boxer into hatred for the pigs, thus reinforcing his political purpose. We now find the pigs disgusting for their cruelty, but of course all the time we are aware that the pigs stand for the corruption power can bring.

It is a book with a design upon us; it has a message, but Orwell would not have got his message across so effectively but for the convention of the animal fable.

Suggested outlines for answers

(3) Trace the growth of the power of the pigs in *Animal Farm*. What lessons does Orwell wish us to draw from this?

(*i*) Pigs naturally more intelligent, so they take control after the Rebellion. They have been learning to read and write in preparation.

(*ii*) Napoleon straightaway drinks the milk, showing his selfishness.

(*iii*) The conflict between Snowball and Napoleon and Snowball's expulsion. With Snowball gone Napoleon has a free rein.

(*iv*) Napoleon changes the Commandments one by one.

(*v*) Through Squealer Napoleon gains control over what the animals think.

(*vi*) Napoleon arranges confessions and trials as warning to the other animals.

(*vii*) The sale of Boxer to Simmonds.

(*viii*) The pigs become human.

(10) Examine the humour of *Animal Farm*. Is it all of the same kind throughout?

(*i*) Discussion of humour involved in seeing animals behave like humans. The effects of exaggeration.

(*ii*) The stupidity of the animals, other than the pigs, is funny, up to a point.

(*iii*) The stupidity of the animals becomes less funny because it means the pigs can do more or less what they like.

(*iv*) Napoleon's trials are without humour.

(*v*) The humour gets more savage as the book goes on. We begin to enjoy laughing *at* the pigs. But our laughter becomes increasingly uncomfortable.

(*vi*) The moral satire of the irony at the close.

Part 5

Suggestions for further reading

The text

ORWELL, GEORGE: *Animal Farm*, Secker & Warburg, London, 1945.
  There is also a paperback edition, published by Penguin Books,
  Harmondsworth, 1951.

Other works by George Orwell

Burmese Days, Secker & Warburg, London, 1934; paperback edition,
  Penguin Books, Harmondsworth, 1972. This novel is based on his
  experiences in the Burmese police.
Collected Essays, Journalism and Letters of George Orwell, edited by
  Sonia Orwell and Ian Angus, second edition, four volumes, Penguin
  Books, Harmondsworth, 1970.
Down and Out in Paris and London, Secker & Warburg, London,
  1933; paperback edition, Penguin Books, Harmondsworth, 1975.
  A documentary account of his life as a dishwasher in Paris and as a
  tramp in Britain.
Homage to Catalonia, Secker & Warburg, London, 1938; paperback
  edition, Penguin Books, Harmondsworth. An account of his
  experiences in the Spanish Civil War.
The Road to Wigan Pier, Secker & Warburg, London, 1937; paperback
  edition, Penguin Books, Harmondsworth, 1971. A documentary
  account of mining communities in the north of England and his
  thoughts on English socialism arising out of his experiences.

General reading

ALDRITT, KEITH: *The Making of George Orwell*, Arnold, London,
  1969. Puts Orwell into the context of his time and examines his
  contribution to modern 'literary culture'.
MEYERS, JEFFREY: *George Orwell: The Critical Heritage*, Routledge
  and Kegan Paul, London, 1975. Has an excellent introduction
  which outlines the development of critical attitudes to Orwell. The
  body of the work consists of selections from Orwell's critics over
  the years.

SANDISON, ALAN: *The Last Man in Europe*, Macmillan, London, 1974. Places Orwell in the English, moral, Protestant tradition.

THOMAS, EDWARD M.: *Orwell*, Oliver & Boyd, Edinburgh and London, 1965. Excellent short study of the range of Orwell's work. Very good on individual works and on style.

THOMSON, DAVID: *Europe Since Napoleon*, Penguin Books, Harmondsworth, 1976. A good general history, invaluable for background information on the 1930s and 1940s.

WILLIAMS, RAYMOND: *Orwell*, Collins/Fontana (paperback edition), Glasgow and London, 1971. Another short study of Orwell; provocative and illuminating, often questioning.

ZWERDLING, ALEX: *Orwell and the Left*, Yale University Press, New Haven and London, 1974. Studies Orwell's relationships with left-wing politics. A very full account.

The author of these notes

ROBERT WELCH is a graduate of University College, Cork, and of the University of Leeds. He is Professor of English and Head of the Department of English, Media and Theatre Studies at the University of Ulster at Coleraine. He has written on English and Anglo-Irish literature and is also the author of York Notes on *Nineteen Eighty-four*. His *Companion to Anglo-Irish Literature* is forthcoming.

York Notes: list of titles

CHINUA ACHEBE
A Man of the People
Arrow of God
Things Fall Apart

EDWARD ALBEE
Who's Afraid of Virginia Woolf?

ELECHI AMADI
The Concubine

ANONYMOUS
Beowulf
Everyman

JOHN ARDEN
Serjeant Musgrave's Dance

AYI KWEI ARMAH
The Beautyful Ones Are Not Yet Born

W. H. AUDEN
Selected Poems

JANE AUSTEN
Emma
Mansfield Park
Northanger Abbey
Persuasion
Pride and Prejudice
Sense and Sensibility

HONORÉ DE BALZAC
Le Père Goriot

SAMUEL BECKETT
Waiting for Godot

SAUL BELLOW
Henderson, The Rain King

ARNOLD BENNETT
Anna of the Five Towns

WILLIAM BLAKE
Songs of Innocence, Songs of Experience

ROBERT BOLT
A Man For All Seasons

ANNE BRONTË
The Tenant of Wildfell Hall

CHARLOTTE BRONTË
Jane Eyre

EMILY BRONTË
Wuthering Heights

ROBERT BROWNING
Men and Women

JOHN BUCHAN
The Thirty-Nine Steps

JOHN BUNYAN
The Pilgrim's Progress

BYRON
Selected Poems

ALBERT CAMUS
L'Etranger (The Outsider)

GEOFFREY CHAUCER
Prologue to the Canterbury Tales
The Clerk's Tale
The Franklin's Tale
The Knight's Tale
The Merchant's Tale
The Miller's Tale
The Nun's Priest's Tale
The Pardoner's Tale
The Wife of Bath's Tale
Troilus and Criseyde

ANTON CHEKOV
The Cherry Orchard

SAMUEL TAYLOR COLERIDGE
Selected Poems

WILKIE COLLINS
The Moonstone
The Woman in White

SIR ARTHUR CONAN DOYLE
The Hound of the Baskervilles

WILLIAM CONGREVE
The Way of the World

JOSEPH CONRAD
Heart of Darkness
Lord Jim
Nostromo
The Secret Agent
Victory
Youth and *Typhoon*

STEPHEN CRANE
The Red Badge of Courage

BRUCE DAWE
Selected Poems

WALTER DE LA MARE
Selected Poems

DANIEL DEFOE
A Journal of the Plague Year
Moll Flanders
Robinson Crusoe

CHARLES DICKENS
A Tale of Two Cities
Bleak House
David Copperfield
Dombey and Son
Great Expectations
Hard Times
Little Dorrit
Nicholas Nickleby
Oliver Twist
Our Mutual Friend
The Pickwick Papers

EMILY DICKINSON
Selected Poems

JOHN DONNE
Selected Poems

THEODORE DREISER
Sister Carrie

GEORGE ELIOT
Adam Bede
Middlemarch
Silas Marner
The Mill on the Floss

T. S. ELIOT
Four Quartets
Murder in the Cathedral
Selected Poems
The Cocktail Party
The Waste Land

J. G. FARRELL
The Siege of Krishnapur

GEORGE FARQUHAR
The Beaux Stratagem

WILLIAM FAULKNER
Absalom, Absalom!
As I Lay Dying
Go Down, Moses
The Sound and the Fury

HENRY FIELDING
Joseph Andrews
Tom Jones

F. SCOTT FITZGERALD
Tender is the Night
The Great Gatsby

E. M. FORSTER
A Passage to India
Howards End

ATHOL FUGARD
Selected Plays

JOHN GALSWORTHY
Strife

MRS GASKELL
North and South

WILLIAM GOLDING
Lord of the Flies
The Inheritors
The Spire

OLIVER GOLDSMITH
She Stoops to Conquer
The Vicar of Wakefield

ROBERT GRAVES
Goodbye to All That

GRAHAM GREENE
Brighton Rock
The Heart of the Matter
The Power and the Glory

THOMAS HARDY
Far from the Madding Crowd
Jude the Obscure
Selected Poems
Tess of the D'Urbervilles
The Mayor of Casterbridge
The Return of the Native
The Trumpet Major
The Woodlanders
Under the Greenwood Tree

L. P. HARTLEY
The Go-Between
The Shrimp and the Anemone

NATHANIEL HAWTHORNE
The Scarlet Letter

SEAMUS HEANEY
Selected Poems

JOSEPH HELLER
Catch-22

ERNEST HEMINGWAY
A Farewell to Arms
For Whom the Bell Tolls
The African Stories
The Old Man and the Sea

GEORGE HERBERT
Selected Poems

HERMANN HESSE
Steppenwolf

BARRY HINES
Kes

HOMER
The Iliad
The Odyssey

ANTHONY HOPE
The Prisoner of Zenda

GERARD MANLEY HOPKINS
Selected Poems

WILLIAM DEAN HOWELLS
The Rise of Silas Lapham

RICHARD HUGHES
A High Wind in Jamaica

THOMAS HUGHES
Tom Brown's Schooldays

ALDOUS HUXLEY
Brave New World

HENRIK IBSEN
A Doll's House
Ghosts
Hedda Gabler

HENRY JAMES
Daisy Miller
The Ambassadors
The Europeans
The Portrait of a Lady
The Turn of the Screw
Washington Square

SAMUEL JOHNSON
Rasselas

BEN JONSON
The Alchemist
Volpone

JAMES JOYCE
A Portrait of the Artist as a Young Man
Dubliners

JOHN KEATS
Selected Poems

RUDYARD KIPLING
Kim

D. H. LAWRENCE
Sons and Lovers
The Rainbow
Women in Love

CAMARA LAYE
L'Enfant Noir

HARPER LEE
To Kill a Mocking-Bird

LAURIE LEE
Cider with Rosie

THOMAS MANN
Tonio Kröger

CHRISTOPHER MARLOWE
Doctor Faustus
Edward II

ANDREW MARVELL
Selected Poems

W. SOMERSET MAUGHAM
Of Human Bondage
Selected Short Stories

GAVIN MAXWELL
Ring of Bright Water

J. MEADE FALKNER
Moonfleet

HERMAN MELVILLE
Billy Budd
Moby Dick

THOMAS MIDDLETON
Women Beware Women

THOMAS MIDDLETON *and* **WILLIAM ROWLEY**
The Changeling

ARTHUR MILLER
Death of a Salesman
The Crucible

JOHN MILTON
Paradise Lost I & II
Paradise Lost IV & IX
Selected Poems

V. S. NAIPAUL
A House for Mr Biswas

SEAN O'CASEY
Juno and the Paycock
The Shadow of a Gunman

GABRIEL OKARA
The Voice

EUGENE O'NEILL
Mourning Becomes Electra

GEORGE ORWELL
Animal Farm
Nineteen Eighty-four

JOHN OSBORNE
Look Back in Anger
WILFRED OWEN
Selected Poems
ALAN PATON
Cry, The Beloved Country
THOMAS LOVE PEACOCK
Nightmare Abbey and *Crotchet Castle*
HAROLD PINTER
The Birthday Party
The Caretaker
PLATO
The Republic
ALEXANDER POPE
Selected Poems
THOMAS PYNCHON
The Crying of Lot 49
SIR WALTER SCOTT
Ivanhoe
Quentin Durward
The Heart of Midlothian
Waverley
PETER SHAFFER
The Royal Hunt of the Sun
WILLIAM SHAKESPEARE
A Midsummer Night's Dream
Antony and Cleopatra
As You Like It
Coriolanus
Cymbeline
Hamlet
Henry IV Part I
Henry IV Part II
Henry V
Julius Caesar
King Lear
Love's Labour Lost
Macbeth
Measure for Measure
Much Ado About Nothing
Othello
Richard II
Richard III
Romeo and Juliet
Sonnets
The Merchant of Venice
The Taming of the Shrew
The Tempest
The Winter's Tale
Troilus and Cressida
Twelfth Night
The Two Gentlemen of Verona
GEORGE BERNARD SHAW
Androcles and the Lion
Arms and the Man
Caesar and Cleopatra
Candida
Major Barbara
Pygmalion
Saint Joan
The Devil's Disciple
MARY SHELLEY
Frankenstein
PERCY BYSSHE SHELLEY
Selected Poems
RICHARD BRINSLEY SHERIDAN
The School for Scandal
The Rivals
WOLE SOYINKA
The Lion and the Jewel
The Road
Three Shorts Plays
EDMUND SPENSER
The Faerie Queene (Book I)

JOHN STEINBECK
Of Mice and Men
The Grapes of Wrath
The Pearl
LAURENCE STERNE
A Sentimental Journey
Tristram Shandy
ROBERT LOUIS STEVENSON
Kidnapped
Treasure Island
Dr Jekyll and Mr Hyde
TOM STOPPARD
Professional Foul
Rosencrantz and Guildenstern are Dead
JONATHAN SWIFT
Gulliver's Travels
JOHN MILLINGTON SYNGE
The Playboy of the Western World
TENNYSON
Selected Poems
W. M. THACKERAY
Vanity Fair
DYLAN THOMAS
Under Milk Wood
EDWARD THOMAS
Selected Poems
FLORA THOMPSON
Lark Rise to Candleford
J. R. R. TOLKIEN
The Hobbit
The Lord of the Rings
CYRIL TOURNEUR
The Revenger's Tragedy
ANTHONY TROLLOPE
Barchester Towers
MARK TWAIN
Huckleberry Finn
Tom Sawyer
JOHN VANBRUGH
The Relapse
VIRGIL
The Aeneid
VOLTAIRE
Candide
EVELYN WAUGH
Decline and Fall
A Handful of Dust
JOHN WEBSTER
The Duchess of Malfi
The White Devil
H. G. WELLS
The History of Mr Polly
The Invisible Man
The War of the Worlds
ARNOLD WESKER
Chips with Everything
Roots
PATRICK WHITE
Voss
OSCAR WILDE
The Importance of Being Earnest
TENNESSEE WILLIAMS
The Glass Menagerie
VIRGINIA WOOLF
Mrs Dalloway
To the Lighthouse
WILLIAM WORDSWORTH
Selected Poems
WILLIAM WYCHERLEY
The Country Wife
W. B. YEATS
Selected Poems

York Handbooks: list of titles